"Tell me what gives y...

"Don't, Benjamin. Don't try to pry to find out any secrets I might have, the kind of woman I am. Trust me when I tell you that you wouldn't like what you uncovered."

"I find that hard to believe."

"Good night, Benjamin," she said, then left the kitchen.

Benjamin deserved better. He deserved more than she'd ever be able to give him. She had no intention of ever loving again.

She didn't want to risk the chance of loss once again. Even with a man like Benjamin. Especially with a man like Benjamin.

She had to keep him out of her heart. She needed him at the moment, but hopefully soon they'd figure out what was going on and she'd be free to leave Black Rock and Benjamin behind.

★★★

Dear Reader,

When I began writing the third book in the Lawmen of Black Rock series, I immediately knew the hero. Benjamin Grayson is a kind man who plays by the rules but has never had a true passion for anything…until he meets the heroine, Edie Burnett.

Benjamin is a middle child, and having married a middle child I knew he would be easygoing and a peacemaker, that it might take him longer to find love and what he wants from life. Once he figured out these things he would be passionate and intense.

When Edie Burnett blows into town and embroils Benjamin in her wacky grandfather's wild ideas, Benjamin doesn't know what hits him. I must confess, I have a bit of the wild and wacky in me and my middle-child husband sometimes doesn't know what's hit him, but he loves me passionately and with an intensity that keeps me a happy woman.

I hope you enjoy *Cowboy Deputy* and I hope you all have that kind of love in your lives.

Happy reading!

Carla Cassidy

CARLA CASSIDY

Cowboy Deputy

ROMANTIC
SUSPENSE

 SILHOUETTE BOOKS

Recycling programs
for this product may
not exist in your area.

ISBN-13: 978-0-373-27709-4

COWBOY DEPUTY

Books by Carla Cassidy

Silhouette Romantic Suspense

CARLA CASSIDY

is an award-winning author who has written more than fifty books for Silhouette Books. In 1995 she won Best Silhouette Romance from *RT Book Reviews* for *Anything for Danny*. In 1998 she also won a Career Achievement Award for Best Innovative Series from *RT Book Reviews*.

Carla believes the only thing better than curling up with a good book to read is sitting down at the computer with a good story to write. She's looking forward to writing many more books and bringing hours of pleasure to readers.

Chapter 1

It was only when she saw the dancing swirl of cherry-colored lights in her rearview mirror that Edie Burnett glanced down at her speedometer. She was going forty miles an hour. As she eased off the gas pedal and pulled to the side of the street in front of a little dress boutique, she caught sight of a sign that indicated the speed limit was twenty-five.

Muttering a curse beneath her breath, she came to a stop at the curb. This was just the icing on the cake of crud that had become her life.

The official car pulled up behind her and she watched in her rearview mirror as the driver got out. Tall and lean, his khaki shirt tugged across broad shoulders as he walked toward her driver window with purposeful strides.

An errant curl of dark hair flopped onto his broad forehead and it only took that single glance in her mirror to know that the man was a hot piece of hunk.

Still, at the moment she didn't much care what he looked like. She needed to figure out the best way to talk him out of giving her a ticket. She wasn't sure she could afford lunch, much less a fine for speeding.

Cute or pathetic? She quickly decided to reach for cute and clueless and then resort to crying if necessary. It had worked for her more than once in the past.

"In a hurry?" His deep, pleasant voice resonated inside her and she looked up to see long-lashed eyes the color of rich, dark chocolate gazing at her.

"Oh, wow, I'm so sorry. I had the radio on and it was a really good song and I guess my speed just kind of got away from me." She gave him a bright bewildered smile. "I didn't notice the speed limit sign until I saw your lights flashing in my rearview mirror."

"But surely you noticed you'd entered the heart of town," he countered.

"I'm such a dunce," she agreed, once again giving him her friendliest grin.

"Driver's license please," he said, no returning smile curving his sexy lips.

Her own smile faltered as she dug into her oversize purse for her wallet. Damn. He was obviously going to give her a ticket. She handed him her license and watched in her mirror as he returned to his car, unable to help but notice that he looked just as good going as he had coming.

Now was the time she'd usually summon up fake tears and hope she could find a soft spot in his heart. But as she stared blindly out the front window the tears that blurred her vision were achingly real.

The past seven months of her life had been an utter nightmare, culminating in the call from somebody here in town that her grandfather needed help.

It had been two years since she'd last seen her grandfather, Walt Tolliver. At that time she'd come back to the small town for her mother's funeral. That particular trip back had been brief and so filled with grief she now scarcely remembered it. Since that time she'd tried to call the old man every weekend, yet in the past six months with her own life falling to pieces, Edie hadn't talked to her grandfather.

A sob escaped her and was quickly followed by another. By the time the deputy returned to her car window, she was blubbering like a baby.

"Hey, there's no need for that," he exclaimed as he held her license out to her. "I'm just going to issue you a warning."

"It's not that," she replied, the words choking out of her between sobs. She grabbed the license and tossed it into the dark recesses of her purse. "It's my life. It sucks. A year ago I was too stupid to live. I thought my creep of a boyfriend loved me and I wanted to do something special for him for his birthday so I gave him my credit card and told him to buy himself the stereo system he'd been drooling over. He bought the stereo all right, and half the store. He maxed out my card and disappeared.

I used most of my savings to pay off the card and then I lost my job."

The words tumbled from her lips as if of their own free will as tears continued to cascade down her cheeks. "Then this morning as I was packing up to drive here, my landlord appeared with a thirty-day notice for me to get out. He's selling the house where I rent an apartment and I have to go."

She suddenly looked up at him, appalled by the gush of her personal problems to the handsome stranger. God, how embarrassing was this? She swiped her cheeks with the back of her hands. "I'm sorry, this isn't your problem. I'm sorry I was speeding and I appreciate you just giving me a warning."

"Are you okay to drive the rest of the way to Walt's house?" he asked.

She nodded. "I'm fine."

He stepped back and motioned for her to pull away from the curb. It was only when she was back on the road that she wondered how he knew she was headed toward her grandfather's place.

How embarrassing, to totally break down in front of a stranger and spill the sordid details of her life. She hadn't cried a tear with each bad thing that had occurred over the past year. It seemed unfathomable that she'd had a mini-breakdown in front of a stranger.

At least she hadn't told him everything. She hadn't told him that the credit card debt Greg had left her with had been the least of the heartache he'd left behind.

She dismissed both Greg and the hot deputy from

her mind as she turned off Main and onto a tree-lined residential street. Black Rock was typical of many small Kansas towns, with the business section taking up two blocks of the main drag surrounded by picturesque side streets lined with mature trees and pleasant, well-kept homes.

When she'd been young she and her mother had often visited her grandparents for a week or so each summer. Her mother and her grandmother would spend much of that time in the kitchen and Walt would entertain Edie by teaching her to play chess, bird-watching in the backyard and gardening.

Those had been some of the happiest days of Edie's life. But when she'd been a teenager, she'd opted for spending time with her friends instead of visiting grandparents. Then the years had slipped away and everything had changed.

Her grandmother had passed away, her mother was gone and now the only family she had left was her Poppy, and according to the brief phone message she'd gotten from somebody here in town, he needed her. The problem was she wasn't in a place where she could be much help to anyone.

As she pulled up in front of the familiar two-story house, her heart fell. Even the forgiving glow of the late afternoon sun couldn't take away the air of neglect that clung to the place.

The lawn needed a good mowing and the house itself screamed for a fresh coat of paint. Weeds had choked the last of the fall flowers in the beds that lined the walkway to the front porch.

She got out of her car and tried to ignore the sense of being overwhelmed. Was he ill? Poppy was seventy-one years old. Was he too old to be living on his own? How was she going to help him when she could barely help herself?

She knocked on the door, hoping he was at least well enough to open it. "Who is there?" The deep voice resounded with energy from the other side of the door.

"Poppy, it's me, Edie."

The door flung open and Edie breathed a sigh of relief at the sight of her grandfather, looking older, but robust and healthy. "What a surprise! If it isn't my favorite girl in the whole wide world." He pulled her into the foyer and into the loving embrace of his arms.

He smelled of cheap cologne and menthol rub, of early autumn air and sweet childhood memories, and as she hugged him back she wondered why she had stayed away for so long.

He finally released her and motioned her to follow him inside. "Come on, then. I need to check on my dinner."

As she followed behind him toward the kitchen she noticed that the inside of the house was neat and tidy and the scent of a roast cooking emanated from the kitchen.

Maybe it had been a cranky neighbor who had called her because of the condition of the exterior of the house and the yard. She couldn't remember the caller giving his name but it was obvious that he had overreacted. Thank God her grandfather seemed fine.

She'd take the next couple of days and mow the lawn, weed the flower beds and maybe get a couple gallons of paint to spruce up the place. She made a commitment to come visit every two months and resume her weekly phone calls.

"Got roast and potatoes for supper," he said as he went to oven and opened the door. "And green beans from the garden. Go on, sit down while I stir these beans and add a little bacon grease."

"Are you expecting company?" she asked, noticing that the table held two place settings. Unless Poppy had suddenly become a psychic, the extra plate hadn't been set for her.

"Benjamin is coming over. He stops by two or three times a week for dinner and some chess." Walt smiled at her. "It will feel like a regular party with you here." He finished stirring the beans and then grabbed a plate from the cabinet and added it to the table.

"I was beginning to think you'd forgotten all about your Poppy," he said with a touch of censure in his voice.

"You know the phone lines go both ways," she replied.

"I know, but I figured if a young girl like you wanted to talk to an old coot like me, you'd call." He eased down in the chair next to her at the table. "What are you now, twenty-three or twenty-four?"

"Twenty-nine, Poppy." Although the past year of her life, she'd made the mistakes of a teenager and suffered a woman's grief.

One of his grizzly gray eyebrows lifted in surprise. "Twenty-nine!" He swiped a hand down his weather-worn face and shook his head. "Seems the past couple of years have plum gotten away from me. That means it's been almost ten years since I lost my Delores and over two years since we lost your mama." For a moment he looked ancient, with sadness darkening his blue eyes and his paper-thin lips turned downward.

The sadness lasted only a moment and then his eyes regained their usual twinkle. "I hope you're going to be here long enough for me to teach you a lesson or two in chess."

She laughed. "I'm not leaving here until I win at least one game."

"Good," he said, obviously delighted. "That means it's going to be a nice long visit."

Although Edie was glad she was here, again she was struck by the thought that he seemed just fine and whoever had called her saying he needed help had definitely overreacted.

He jumped out of his chair and walked over to the oven and opened the door. "Benjamin should be here soon and we'll eat. Are you hungry?"

"Starving," she replied. Her lunch had been a bag of chips she'd eaten in the car. "Is there anything I can do to help?"

"There are a couple of nice tomatoes in the

refrigerator. If you want to, you can slice them up and put them on the table."

As she sliced the tomatoes, they chatted mostly about the past, playing a game of *remember when* that created warm fuzzies in Edie's heart.

She shouldn't have stayed away for so long. Poppy was the only family she had left in the world. Her home in Topeka was just a three-hour drive to Black Rock but somehow her personal drama and heartbreak had taken over and the last thing on her mind had been her Poppy.

"You'll like Benjamin," Poppy said as he took the roaster out of the oven and set it on hot pads in the center of the table. "He's a good guy and a mean chess player."

And probably eighty years old, Edie mentally thought, although she was grateful her grandfather had a friend for company. Maybe this big house was just too much for Poppy. Maybe it was time for him to think about an apartment or someplace where he didn't have to worry about maintenance and upkeep. Time to talk about that later, she thought as the doorbell rang.

"That should be Benjamin," Walt said and left the kitchen to get the door.

Edie wiped off the countertop and then pasted a smile on her face as Walt came back into the kitchen. The smile fell as she saw who followed at his heels, not an old, gray-haired man with stooped shoulders and rheumy eyes, but rather the very hot deputy who had pulled her over and witnessed her mini-breakdown.

"Edie, this here is my friend, Benjamin Grayson. Benjamin, this is my granddaughter who surprised me this evening with a visit," Walt said.

"Hello, Edie, it's nice to meet you." He stepped forward and held out a hand, obviously deciding to play it as if he'd never seen her before.

He'd looked great earlier in his khaki uniform but now with worn tight jeans hugging his long lean legs and a blue cotton shirt clinging to his broad shoulders, he was pure sin walking.

"Nice to meet you, too," she replied as she gave his hand a short, curt shake.

"Go on, sit down," Walt said. "Let's eat before the roast gets cold."

Edie slid into a chair at the table and tried not to notice the clean, male scent mingling with a woodsy cologne that wafted from Benjamin.

He might have smelled good and he might have looked great and in another place and time she might have been interested in him. But Edie had sworn off relationships and men and sex for the rest of her life. Besides, her intention was to be in Black Rock for only two or three days.

As the men joined her at the table and filled their plates, Walt and Benjamin made small talk about the weather and the forecast for a harsh winter to come.

Although Edie was glad she'd gotten the phone call that had prompted her to come for a visit, she still didn't see any real issue where her Poppy was concerned.

"Any word on that missing girl?" Walt asked.

Benjamin shook his head. "Nothing. It's like she vanished into midair."

"Missing girl?" Edie looked at Benjamin curiously.

"Her name is Jennifer Hightower, a twenty-two-year-old who went missing three weeks ago," Benjamin replied.

"And she's not the only missing girl in town," Walt said. "Benjamin's own sister went missing over two months ago."

Edie saw the darkness that crawled into Benjamin's eyes as he nodded. "That's right, but surely we can think of something more pleasant to talk about while we eat." There was a note of finality in his tone that indicated this particular subject was closed.

Walt immediately began to talk about the fall festival the town was planning in the next month. As Edie ate, she found that her focus tugged again and again to Benjamin.

His face was tanned as if he spent a lot of time outdoors rather than inside at a desk or seated in a patrol car. He had nice features, a no-nonsense slight jut to his chin, a straight nose and lips that looked soft and very kissable.

There was no question that she was curious about his sister, felt a tinge of empathy as she imagined what it must be like to have a family member missing.

Edie didn't know about missing family members, but she was intimate with grief, knew the sharp stab of loss, the ache that never quite went away.

She could only assume that Benjamin wasn't married

and she questioned why a handsome man like him would choose to spend a couple nights a week playing chess with an old man.

"How long are you planning to visit?" he asked.

With those gorgeous, long-lashed eyes focused intently on her, a small burst of unwanted heat ignited in the very pit of her stomach.

"Just a couple days or so," she replied, grateful her voice sounded remarkably normal. "I need to get back home and take care of some things." And he knew exactly what those things were because she'd spewed them out in a mist of tears when he'd pulled her over.

"You still managing that restaurant?" Poppy asked.

She hesitated and then shook her head. "Unfortunately a couple weeks ago I showed up at the restaurant and found a padlock on the door and a note that said the place was out of business." She tamped down the residual anger that rose up inside her each time she thought of that day. There had been no warning to any of the employees, no hint that the place was in trouble.

"So, have you found a new job?" Poppy eyed her worriedly.

"Not yet, but when I get back home I'm sure I won't have any problems finding something," she assured him with a quick smile. The last thing she wanted was for him to worry about her.

Thankfully dinner went quickly and as Poppy stood to clear the table, Edie shooed him away. "You two go on and play your chess. I'll take care of the cleanup."

"I won't argue with you. I like the cooking but hate the cleanup," Poppy said.

"I could help. It would only take a minute," Benjamin said.

Edie shook her head. "I've got it under control." The last thing she wanted was to be butting elbows with him over the sink. He was too big and too sexy for her and she didn't want him close enough that she could smell him, feel his body heat.

She breathed a sigh of relief as the two men left the kitchen and disappeared into the living room. It took her only minutes to store the leftovers in the refrigerator and then stack the plates for washing.

There was no dishwasher and as she got the dish drainer rack from the cabinet, she remembered all the times she'd stood at this sink and helped her grandmother wash dishes.

It hadn't been a chore; it had been a chance to talk about the day, about the weather, about life with a woman Edie had considered wise and loving.

The last time Edie had been here she'd been thirteen years old and madly in love with a boy named Darrin. It had been a case of unrequited love. Darrin had preferred video games to girls.

"It's not a mistake to love," her grandmother had told her. "But you need to love smart. Choose a man who has the capacity to love you back, a man who can make you feel as if you're the most important person in the world."

As Edie washed and rinsed the dishes, she wondered

what her grandmother would say about the mess Edie had made of her life. She had definitely loved stupid, choosing to give her heart to a man who not only didn't have the capacity to love her back, but also had all the character of a rock. The price she'd paid for loving stupidly had been enormous and she'd been left with the determination to never put her heart in jeopardy again.

A burst of deep male laughter came from the living room as she placed the last dish in the drainer. It sounded like the two of them were enjoying their game.

Darkness had fallen outside and Edie realized she hadn't brought in her suitcase from the car. As she entered the living room both men looked up from the chessboard. "What are you doing, girl?" Poppy asked. "Come sit and watch a master at work." He gave her a grin that twinkled in his eyes.

She returned his smile. "I gather from the smug look on your face that you're winning."

"I've been playing him a couple nights a week for the past six months and I have yet to win a game," Benjamin said.

His gaze slid down the length of her, the quick once-over that a man might give a woman he found attractive.

She felt the heat of his gaze and quickly moved toward the front door. "I'm just going to get my suitcase from the car."

"Need any help?" Benjamin asked.

She quickly shook her head. "Thanks, but I can get

it." She scooted out the front door and into the cool September evening air.

For a moment she stood on the porch and stared up at the night sky. Here in Black Rock the stars seemed brighter, closer than they did in Topeka.

"Make a wish, sugar," her grandmother would tell her whenever the two of them had sat on the porch and gazed upward.

Edie reached up and grabbed the small charm that hung on the gold chain around her neck. The gold was cool in her fingers but warmed quickly as she held it tight.

There was only one wish she'd like to make and she knew it was one that could never come true. She released her hold on the charm and headed to her car in the driveway.

Behind her car was parked a large black pickup she knew must belong to Benjamin. Funny, she would assume he was more the sweet little sports car type than the big, bruising truck.

She'd packed light and grabbed the small suitcase and overnight bag from her backseat, then headed inside the house. She heard no sound from the living room. Apparently the current chess game was intense enough that both men were concentrating.

She carried the suitcase up the stairs, the third and seventh steps creaking beneath her weight as they had when she'd been a child. She entered the last bedroom at the end of the hall, the room where she'd always stayed when she and her mother had come for a visit.

The dusty pink paint on the wall and the pink floral spread covering the double bed brought another wave of memories.

Every night that she'd slept here she'd been tucked into bed lovingly not only by her mother, but also by her grandmother. And often Poppy would come upstairs to sneak her a cookie or a little bowl of popcorn. In this house, she'd always felt loved like nowhere else on earth.

It took her only minutes to stow her items in the dresser and closet, then she headed back downstairs where it sounded like the chess game had ended.

As she entered the living room, Benjamin and Poppy got up from the small game table. "He beat me both games," Benjamin said. He smiled at Edie, a warm, sexy smile that once again fluttered a faint heat through her veins.

"Maybe you and Edie could play a few games together, you know, practice so eventually you can beat the master." Poppy grinned.

Benjamin laughed. "I'd love to hang around and play a game of chess with Edie, but unfortunately I've got some reports that need to be written before morning."

The twinkle in Poppy's eyes faded as he looked at Benjamin seriously. "You know how to find those girls. Find the aliens and you'll find out what happened to that Hightower young woman and your sister."

"Aliens?" Edie looked from her grandfather to Benjamin with curiosity.

Poppy nodded. "Space aliens. I keep telling Benjamin

and his brothers that they've landed here in Black Rock and until we get them rounded up, nobody is safe."

A sick feeling swept through Edie as she stared at her grandfather, hoping to see the familiar twinkle of a joke in his eyes. But there was no twinkle—only a faint tinge of fear coupled with the determination of an intergalactic warrior. And then she knew why somebody had called her to check on her Poppy. It was because he was losing his mind.

Chapter 2

Benjamin saw the dismay that swept over Edie's features at Walt's words. She was a pretty woman and he knew her statistics from looking at her license. She was five foot four and weighed 117 pounds. Her hair was auburn and her eyes were green.

But those statistics didn't begin to really describe the woman who stood before him. Yes, her short curly hair was auburn, but it shone with a luster that made his fingers itch with the need to touch. *Green* was too ordinary a word to describe her eyes, which sparkled with tiny shards of glittering gold.

The orange sweater she wore complemented the burnished highlights in her hair and intensified the color of her eyes. Something about her stirred him in a way he hadn't been stirred in a very long time.

"I'll walk you out," she said, casting a meaningful look at him.

"Walt, as always, thanks for the meal and the chess game," Benjamin said.

"Thanks for the company," Walt replied, obviously unaware that his previous words had upset his granddaughter. "Edie, you can pull your car into the garage. I sold my car a year ago. I got tired of paying for insurance."

Edie nodded. "Thanks, Poppy, I'll do that."

As Benjamin walked out with Edie, he caught a whiff of her perfume, something subtle and spicy that reminded him of tangy fall air and cinnamon.

"I'm the one who called you," he said when they were far enough away from the front door that Walt wouldn't hear. "I've been worried about him."

In the illumination from a nearby streetlight, he could see the confusion on her pretty face. "I didn't catch the name of the person who'd called me and once I got here I thought maybe it was just a cranky neighbor upset because the yard needs some work. He seemed so normal."

"He appears to be normal in every way except for the little issue that he thinks space aliens are trying to take over Black Rock. It wouldn't be a big problem but he's often out in the middle of the night alien hunting and I'm afraid he'll get hit by a car or fall down someplace where nobody will be able to help him."

"How long has this been going on?" she asked. She still looked overwhelmed by this news and as he remembered the things she'd told him when he'd pulled her over for speeding, he had a crazy desire to take her into his arms and assure her that everything was going to be all right.

Instead he rocked back on his heels and frowned thoughtfully. "About six months. My brothers and I have tried to assure him that there are no space aliens in town, but he's adamant in his belief and gets downright cranky when you try to tell him different. Look, I'd recommend you take him into his doctor and get a full checkup done. Maybe this is some sort of a medical issue."

"I guess that's as good a place to start as anywhere," she replied. "Well, thanks for all your help with him. I guess I'll see you around over the next couple of days, but hopefully not in my rearview mirror with your lights spinning."

He grinned at her. "As long as you're not a fast woman, we won't have any problems in that area. But I can't promise I won't follow you just because I think you're pretty." Someplace deep inside he recognized he was flirting a little bit.

She must have realized it, too. But her eyes cooled and she took a step back from him. "I am a fast woman, probably way too fast for a small-town deputy."

He wasn't sure who was more surprised by her response, him or her. Her lush lips compressed as she frowned once again. "Thanks again for you help. See you around."

She turned and headed back to the house in short quick steps that swayed her shapely hips. Benjamin watched until she disappeared behind the front door and then released a sigh as he got into his truck.

He had no idea what had possessed him to attempt a little flirt with her. It was obvious by her response he wasn't very good at it. Still, her cool response had surprised him.

Since his brothers Tom and Caleb had hooked up with their soul mates, Benjamin had become the toast of the town when it came to the single women. But all the women who were interested in him left him cold.

He'd been cold since his sister, Brittany, had disappeared over two months ago. Tom, his oldest brother and the sheriff of Black Rock, still held out hope that she would be found alive and well, but even though Benjamin never said anything out loud, as each day had passed with no word from her, he'd lost hope of ever seeing his little sister again.

As he backed out of Walt's driveway, he tried to ignore the stab of grief that always pierced his heart when he thought of his missing sister.

And now they had another one missing. Tom was reluctant to tie the two disappearances together, but Benjamin had a bad feeling about the whole thing. He was afraid Black Rock was in for dark days, and the darkness had nothing to do with Walt's imaginary space aliens.

As he headed for the ranch his thoughts returned to Edie Burnett. For a minute as he'd seen her tears after he'd pulled her over, he'd thought she was faking them to get out of a ticket.

Old Mabel Tredway did it on a regular basis. The eighty-two-year-old woman shouldn't be behind the wheel of a car and whenever Benjamin pulled her over for crossing the center line or going a little too fast, she wept like a baby. But the one time he'd given her a ticket, the fake tears had stopped on a dime and she'd cussed him, his dead mama and all the cattle on his ranch.

However, Edie's tears had been real and as she'd burped up the details of her life with each sob, he had decided not to write the ticket.

She had enough to deal with in deciding what to do with Walt. Benjamin and his lawmen brothers had come to the end of their rope with the old man. Nobody wanted to see anything bad happen to him, but they all felt it was just a matter of time before he got hurt.

As he pulled into the gates that led to the family homestead, he felt the familiar sense of peace the place always brought to him. The house itself was an architectural anomaly. What had started as a simple two-bedroom ranch had become a sprawling complex as rooms were added with each birth of a child.

There was also a small cottage just behind the house where Margaret Kintell, a sixty-eight-year-old widow, lived. Margaret had worked as a housekeeper for the Grayson family for as long as Benjamin could remember. Her husband, John, had worked as a ranch hand until he'd passed away several years ago, and even though Benjamin had encouraged Margaret to retire she insisted that her job was still taking care of the Grayson children.

Unfortunately Benjamin was the only Grayson child still living in the family home and he wasn't exactly a child at thirty years old. His brothers Tom and Caleb lived in town. Brittany had been living in town at the time of her disappearance and Jacob was holed up in a small cabin nestled in a grove of trees on the ranch property.

The porch light was on so he knew Margaret was probably still in the house rather than in her little cottage. As he walked through the front door, the scent of apples and cinnamon filled his nose and Tiny came running toward him, barking a happy greeting.

"Hi, Tiny." He bent down on his haunches to pet the mixed-breed mutt who had stolen his heart six months ago. "Margaret?" he called as he stood. As he walked through the living room toward the kitchen, Tiny followed close at his feet.

She greeted him in the doorway and gestured him into a chair at the table. "Go on, now, sit down. I made fresh apple cobbler and I know that nutcase Walt probably didn't feed you good and proper."

Benjamin smiled and eased down at the table. "Actually, he had a very nice roast and potatoes for dinner." Margaret had been mad at Walt since last year's fall festival when his apple pie had beaten out hers for a blue ribbon.

She harrumphed as she scooped up a healthy serving of the cobbler into a bowl. "Probably got the recipe from one of those space aliens of his. I don't know why you have taken that man under your wing. You're too soft,

Benjamin. That's always been your problem. All Walt Tolliver needs is a stern talking-to." She placed the bowl in front of him and then went to the refrigerator and pulled out the jug of milk.

"Maybe his granddaughter can talk some sense into him. She arrived in town today."

"Really?" Margaret placed a glass of milk in front of him and then sat across from him. "That would be Julie's girl."

"Edie," Benjamin replied. "Her name is Edie Burnett."

"That's right. Julie married that no-account Kevin Burnett. He was a drinker, that one, and a womanizer. The marriage lasted just long enough for Julie to get pregnant. It was a shame, her dying like that in a car accident. So, what's Edie like?"

Hot. With tantalizing eyes and a body that could make a man weak in the knees. He spooned some of the apple cobbler in his mouth in an effort to think of a more reasonable response.

"She didn't seem to know what's been going on with Walt and when she realized he thought Black Rock was being invaded by space aliens, she seemed a little overwhelmed by it all," he finally replied.

"She in town to stay?"

"No. I imagine she'll just be here long enough to figure out what needs to be done with Walt and then she'll go back home."

"What's she like? Julie was a pretty woman and sweet as that cobbler."

"She's nice-looking," Benjamin conceded, "but I think she might have a little bite to her." He thought about how her gaze had frosted over when he'd attempted a little light flirtation.

If he were a man who liked a challenge, he might have pursued a little more flirting just to see if he could melt that frost. But Benjamin was a man who'd never felt enough passion to work too hard for anything. Except this ranch.

"She's got her work cut out for her in straightening out that old man," Margaret said as she rose from the table. "I'm going to head to my place. It's time for this old broad to call it a night."

Benjamin smiled. "Good night, Margaret." The old woman had the heart of an angel and the saltiness of a sailor, but she helped to keep the ranch and Benjamin's life running smoothly.

Once she was gone the silence of the house pressed in on him. Growing up with all his siblings in the house, he'd longed for silence.

But lately the silence in his life had felt oppressive, ushering in a loneliness he'd never felt before. His brother Jacob had closed himself off in the cabin in some form of self-imposed isolation. Brittany was missing and Tom and Caleb now had beautiful bright women to fill the silences in their lives.

He got up from the table and carried his bowl and glass to the sink. As he rinsed the dishes and placed them in the dishwasher, he thought of all the things he needed to get done in the next couple days while he was off-duty.

Of course, the law enforcement team in Black Rock was so small that all of the men were often called in on their time off. He left the kitchen and doused the light, then headed toward the master bedroom.

As always, when the silence pressed in the heaviest, his thoughts turned to Brittany. A little over two months without a word, without a clue as to what happened to her. They'd found her car hidden in an abandoned barn a month ago and it was at that moment that any hope he might have entertained in seeing his sister alive again had died.

With intentions of rising before dawn to start the catch-up on chores around the ranch, he shucked his jeans and shirt and got ready for bed. Tiny sat next to the bed and looked up at him expectantly.

"You know you have your own bed to sleep in," he said to the dog, who cocked his head as if he didn't understand. Benjamin pointed to the dog bed in the corner. "Go on, get to bed."

Tiny remained in place for a long moment and then finally slunk slowly to his bed. He got in and then looked at Benjamin with mournful brown eyes.

"I don't know why you look so sad," Benjamin said. "We both know you'll be curled up in my bed at my feet before morning."

Minutes later, as he eased down onto his king-size bed, his thoughts returned to Edie Burnett. She'd been quiet during the meal but he had a feeling quiet wasn't really in her character.

He burrowed down and closed his eyes. It was just his luck that the first woman in a long time who had stirred something inside him was only in town for a couple days.

From what she'd told him, she'd have a mess on her hands when she got back home. She had to find a new job and another place to live. He didn't want to think about what she was going to do if Walt's problem wasn't a quick fix.

He drifted off to sleep with visions of lush lips and green eyes playing in his dreams and was awakened some time later by the ringing of his phone on the nightstand.

He was awake instantly, his heart drumming a rapid beat. He glanced at the clock as he fumbled in the dark for the receiver. Just after midnight. Nothing ever good came from middle-of-the-night phone calls.

"Yeah," he answered as he sat up.

"It's me," his brother Tom said. "I'm at the hospital. Somebody beat the hell out of Walt Tolliver and he won't talk to anyone but you."

"I'm on my way." Benjamin hung up as he climbed out of bed. As he pulled on his clothes he wondered what the hell had happened to Walt and where the hell Edie had been.

Edie rolled over and looked at the clock next to her bed. Just before midnight and she still hadn't managed to fall asleep. When she'd come back into the house after Benjamin had left, she'd grabbed her keys and then moved her car into the garage. When she'd returned she'd wanted to ask Poppy more questions about the space aliens he thought were trying to take over Black Rock, but she was afraid to indulge the delusion. She was hoping to talk to his doctor and ask how she should handle the situation.

Even if she'd wanted to talk to him about it, the opportunity didn't arise. Immediately after, Poppy had gone to sleep in the bedroom just off the living room.

She'd climbed the stairs to her room, but knew that sleep would be elusive. She'd taken a long hot shower and tried not to think about Benjamin Grayson. But thoughts of the man kept intruding.

She'd been rude to him with her little remark about being too fast for a small-time deputy, but even though she'd just met him, she'd felt an inexplicable need to distance him from her. His smile had been far too warm, his eyes had been too brown and for just a moment, she'd been afraid that he might make her forget that she'd sworn off men for the rest of her life.

She'd been an accident waiting to happen when she'd met Greg. Reeling with grief over her mother's unexpected death, she'd met him in a bar two weeks after the funeral. It had been love at third drink.

They'd dated for two months before he'd moved in with her and she realized now she'd been far too naive, hadn't asked enough questions and instead had believed everything he'd told her about himself.

They'd talked of marriage and children and he'd filled the loneliness that the absence of her mother had left behind. He'd told her that he was an entrepreneur between projects and that his money was tied up in his latest endeavor. God, she'd been such a fool.

One thing was clear, she didn't need anyone in her life. When she got back home she'd focus on finding a new job, a new place to live and cleaning up her messes. She would be just fine all alone for the rest of her life.

She must have fallen asleep because she knew she was dreaming. Pain ripped her body, but it was a pain tempered with a sense of joy. A bright lamp nearly blinded her as the pain intensified. A murmur of voices took on an urgency that was suddenly terrifying and at the same time a bald-headed man wearing a doctor's mask glared at her with accusation and a phone began to ring.

She awoke with a gasp, the taste of overwhelming grief and crushing guilt thick in her mouth. Disoriented for a moment, she looked around the moonlit room. Then she remembered where she was and that the phone she'd heard in her dream was actually the phone ringing in the house.

As it rang again…and again, she realized Poppy either didn't hear it or didn't intend to answer it. She looked at the clock. Twelve forty-five. Whoever was calling was persistent, for the ringing didn't stop.

She jumped out of bed and left her room. Flipping on the hall light, she ran down the stairs and grabbed the receiver of the phone in the living room.

"Hello," she said half-breathlessly.

"It's me, Benjamin." His deep voice sounded irritated. "I'm here at the hospital with Walt."

"What?" Confusion sifted through her as she looked at the closed door of Poppy's bedroom. "But he went to bed earlier."

"Apparently he went out. Somebody beat him up and he managed to flag down a car that brought him to the hospital. He's going to be all right, but I think you should be here."

"I'm on my way. Where is the hospital?"

"Go straight down Main to Chestnut and turn left. It's about halfway down the second block. You can't miss it."

She murmured a goodbye and then raced back up the stairs to get dressed. Her heart beat an uneven tattoo as she thought of somebody beating up Poppy.

Why, oh, why, had he left the house in the middle of the night? This delusion of his about space aliens obviously had a dark undertone.

Within minutes she was dressed and in her car creeping down the darkened Main Street, seeking Chestnut. Benjamin had sounded angry, as if it were somehow her fault that Poppy had been out wandering the streets. What did he expect her to do? Strap the man into bed at night?

She found the hospital, a two-story brick building with a large parking area near the emergency room entrance. She easily found a parking space, and as she hurried into the door she prayed that Benjamin was right and Poppy was going to be okay.

Once again she kicked herself for staying away for so long. She didn't need Poppy, but it was obvious he needed her. The first person she saw when she walked into the waiting room was Benjamin.

His dark, thick hair was tousled as if he'd just climbed out of bed, making him look even sexier than she remembered. He jumped up from the plastic chair he'd been in as he saw her.

"Where is he?" she asked.

"Where were you?" he countered, his shoulders rigid with tension. "Didn't you know he had gone out?"

"He went to bed just after you left. I went upstairs to go to sleep, as well. What was I supposed to do, tie a little silver bell around his neck so I'd know if he was on the move?" she asked belligerently.

The tension slid off his shoulders and he smiled. "You'd need a ball and chain because I'm afraid he'd be able to get a little silver bell off." He rocked back on his heels and slid a hand through his unruly hair. "Sorry, I didn't mean to come at you like that."

"And I'm sorry I didn't have a ball and chain on Poppy," she replied, reluctantly charmed by his apologetic smile. "How is he? Can I see him?"

Benjamin nodded. "He's been waiting for you. He refused to talk to me until you got here. Come on, I'll take you to him." He placed his fingers just beneath her elbow, and she felt the warmth of the touch burning her through the sweater she'd pulled on. She tore her arm away from him.

What was it about this man that made her feel defensive and prickly? Maybe she was overly sensitive to him because he was the least of her problems. She had a life in Topeka that was in complete and total chaos and a crazy grandfather in Black Rock that she somehow had to fix before she could go home.

She heard Poppy before they reached the exam room. "I'm fine. I just need to go home and rest a bit." His voice held the raspy edge of frustration.

As she and Benjamin stepped into the exam room Edie's breath whooshed out of her at the sight of Poppy, who sat upright on the examining table. One of his eyes was blackened and swollen shut and his jaw held a massive bruise that appeared to grow darker as she stared at him.

"Oh, Poppy," she exclaimed, her heart squeezing tight in her chest. "What happened?"

He shifted positions and winced. "One of the bastards caught me."

"Where were you, Walt?" Benjamin asked.

The doctor, an older man with a receding hairline and a kind smile, held up a hand to halt any questioning. "Before we get into that, I'm Dr. Drake. I've been Walt's doctor for the past twenty years." He held out a hand to Edie, who introduced herself.

"Other than what's obvious, what are his injuries?" she asked.

"A couple of cracked ribs and a lot of bruising along

his left side. I'd like to keep him here under observation for a night or two."

Edie breathed a sigh of relief at the doctor's words, but Walt took exception. "I don't need to stay overnight. I want my own bed in my own house."

"Walt, as your doctor I'm afraid I'm going to have to insist," Dr. Drake said firmly. "You took quite a beating and I wouldn't be doing my job if I just let you out of here without running a few more tests."

The mutiny on Poppy's face eased into something resembling resignation. "I'm not going to wear one of those damn gowns and this place better have cable television. And I want a pretty nurse."

Dr. Drake smiled. "I think we can handle all that. Now I'll just get out of here and let Benjamin conduct his investigation."

"Dr. Drake, before I leave, I'd like to have a word with you in private," Edie said.

He nodded. "I'll be in my office at the end of the hall, and if I'm not there just grab a nurse and have her hunt me down." He left the room and Edie turned back to Poppy as Benjamin stepped closer to the bed.

"Where were you, Walt?" he asked again.

"Out by the cemetery. I thought that might be a hot spot for those creatures and damned if I wasn't right. I was only there about an hour when one of them showed up. Either I made a sound or those suckers have some kind of extrasensory stuff 'cause even though I was hiding behind a bush, he came tearing after me." He looked from Benjamin to Edie. "I think it's best if you leave town, Edie. Those creatures are violent and this town isn't a safe place anymore."

"I'm not going anywhere, Poppy," she replied. "At least not until I know you're safe and well."

"This space alien, what did he look like?" Benjamin asked.

"Like an alien," Walt exclaimed, seeming to get more agitated with each question.

"Poppy, you need to be more specific," Edie replied. "Was he little and green?"

Poppy shot her a look as if she'd lost her mind. "He wasn't some damn cartoon Martian. I couldn't tell much what he looked like. He was wearing all black. His face didn't have a nose or mouth, just big eyes."

"Where exactly in the cemetery were you?" Benjamin had pulled out a small notepad to jot down the pertinent information.

"I was hiding behind that big burning bush at the entrance and the alien was just inside the gate."

"What was he doing?" Benjamin asked.

"Just walking," Walt replied.

On and on the questions went. To Benjamin's credit he didn't lose patience even when Walt got cranky and insisted they needed to call in more law enforcement for the small town.

When the nurse came in to move him from emergency into one of the regular rooms, Edie and Benjamin were shooed out. Edie gave Poppy a gentle kiss on the top of the head and after promising to visit him the next morning, she and Benjamin left the room.

"You didn't get much to go on," she said to Benjamin as they walked down the hall toward the doctor's office. Nervous energy jangled inside her. She'd managed to hold it together in front of Poppy, but she felt perilously close to losing it now.

"I'm sure it wasn't a space invader on a nefarious mission, but *somebody* hurt Walt and I intend to find the person responsible," he said with an intensity that somehow calmed her.

"Why would somebody want to hurt him like that? He's an old man. He's not a threat to anyone." She was horrified to feel the ominous burn of tears in her eyes. God, she'd only been with Benjamin three times and she refused to be in tears yet again.

"Are you all right?" he asked. There was a softness in his eyes, a gentle but steady light that made her want to fall into it. He raised a hand, as if to touch her hair or cheek, but dropped it as she stiffened her back and took a step away from him. Someplace buried in her mind she recognized that this man was definitely dangerous to her.

"I need to speak to Dr. Drake. Please keep me updated on the investigation." Without waiting for his reply, she turned and hurried down the hall, away from him…away from temptation.

Chapter 3

The Black Rock Memorial Cemetery was located about two miles from Walt's home. It was a peaceful plot of land, shady with large trees and with several stone benches amid the headstones.

The grass was neatly mown and the flower beds without a weed. The place was maintained by Josh Willoughby who lived in a small house next to the cemetery. He was an affable man who worked at the feed store and took care of the cemetery on the weekends and on his days off.

Benjamin's parents were here. They'd been killed in a helicopter accident six years ago and as Benjamin approached the front gate, he made a mental note to stop by their graves before he left.

The bush that Walt had told him he'd hidden behind

was next to the front gate, a burning bush that had fully flamed into red leaves with the fall air.

The grass was too short and dry to show any signs of the struggle that had taken place between Walt and his space alien. He bent down on one knee next to the bush and began to comb the grass with his gloved hand, looking for some sort of evidence that might help identify Walt's attacker.

As he worked he couldn't help but think about Edie. She'd been foremost in his thoughts since he'd left her at the hospital near dawn.

He'd been impressed by how she'd handled the situation at the hospital. She'd remained calm and patient with Walt even when he'd gotten downright cantankerous.

It was only as they'd stepped out of the room that he saw a crack in her composure. She'd looked small and lost and overwhelmed by everything that was going on. Benjamin had fought the impulse to pull her into his arms and hold her until somehow her world was magically set right.

His family teased him about his penchant for picking up strays. Dogs and cats and people needing help always seemed to find their way to Benjamin.

But his crazy attraction to Edie Burnett had nothing to do with his desire to help her through a tough situation. The very scent of her excited him, her nearness half stole his breath away and her mouth seemed to beckon for a taste. He was like a teenager in heat and wasn't quite sure what to do with his desire for her.

He'd wanted to kiss her, right there in the hospital hallway. He'd wanted to pull her up against his body and wrap his arms around her and hold her until that frightened, lost look in her eyes changed to desire.

It was a new feeling for him, the instant chemistry he felt toward her and one he was reluctant to deny.

All thoughts of Edie flew out of his head as his hand touched something metal. He pulled the item from the grass and gazed at it thoughtfully. It appeared to be part of a key chain, a flat black circle with the initial *A* in silver in the center.

He placed it in a small evidence bag. There was no way of knowing if it might have come off Walt's attacker or had been dropped by somebody else at another time.

"Problems?"

The deep voice coming from just behind Benjamin spun him up and around, his hand automatically reaching for his gun. "Jeez, Josh, you scared the hell out of me," he said as he relaxed. "I figured you were at work."

"It's my day off. I saw you skulking around and wondered if there was a problem."

"Walt Tolliver got the tar beat out of him here last night."

Josh frowned and hitched up his jeans around his bulging belly. He was a big man, an inch taller than Benjamin's six feet and at least fifty pounds heavier. "I've been trying to keep an extra eye out here lately but last night me and the wife went to bed early."

"So you didn't see or hear anything?"

"Only thing I heard was Marylou's snores. The woman sounded like a freight train with brake problems last night, not that I'd like you to mention it to her." He gave Benjamin a pained smile.

"Why have you been keeping an extra eye out here?" Benjamin asked.

"A few times over the past couple weeks I thought I saw lights. I figured it was probably kids fooling around. There was never any damage or any sign that they were there in the mornings so I wasn't sure if it was just my imagination."

"The next time you think you see something, you call the sheriff's office," Benjamin said.

"Is Walt okay?" Josh asked.

Benjamin nodded. "Banged up, but he'll survive."

"He wasn't able to tell you who attacked him?"

"Don't ask," Benjamin said darkly.

A slow grin swept over Josh's broad face. "Let me guess, it was a space invader."

Benjamin nodded. "I'm headed over to the hospital from here to see if he can give me more details this morning than he was able to last night."

"Good luck with that," Josh said. "I'm going back home. Just call if you need anything else from me."

Benjamin watched as the big man lumbered back in the direction of his house, then Benjamin walked toward his parents' graves.

He didn't visit here often. In truth Benjamin had been closer to his siblings than he had been to his mother and father. His parents had loved to travel and once their kids all got old enough to fend for themselves, they were often away on one adventure or another.

He stood at the foot of their graves and wondered if they were both whirling around in spiritual unrest with Brittany's disappearance and Jacob's isolation from life.

Brittany's case had come to a painful standstill due to a lack of leads. As far as Jacob, Benjamin held out hope that eventually Jacob would tell him why he'd quit his job with the FBI and closed himself off from the world.

It was just after noon when he left the cemetery and decided to stop for lunch before going to the hospital. As he walked into the café he spied his brothers Tom and Caleb in one of the booths.

As he walked toward where they were seated, he nodded to Larry Norwood, the town's newest vet, and raised a hand to Billy Jefferson, a neighboring rancher.

"We were just sitting here wondering if our resident alien buster had been successful in his hunt," Caleb teased as Benjamin slid in next to him. "Any sight of the little green men?"

"I'll have you know that Walt specifically said that the alien wasn't a cartoon Martian. He wasn't sure what planet the aliens are from."

"It was somebody from this planet who beat him up," Tom said, his features stern. "And I want that person found and charged. I don't like things like that happening in my town."

Benjamin knew how personally Tom took the safety of the residents of Black Rock. It was what made him a respected and beloved sheriff. "I spoke to Josh," Benjamin said. "He mentioned that he thinks maybe kids have been hanging out at the cemetery after hours."

"I'm not surprised," Caleb said. "Halloween is only weeks away. There's nothing better than taking a girl to the cemetery and scaring her with ghost stories that make her squeal in fear and jump right into your arms."

"Does Portia know you hang out in the cemetery and scare girls?" Benjamin asked with a wry grin.

Caleb smiled. "She was the girl I was scaring in the cemetery."

Portia Perez and Caleb had been high-school sweethearts who had broken up when Portia had gone to college. Recently the two had gotten back together again and seemed more in love with each other than ever.

"What about Walt's granddaughter? What's her name?" Tom asked.

To Benjamin's surprise he felt his cheeks warm. "Edie. Edie Burnett."

"What's she like?" Caleb asked curiously.

Benjamin shrugged. "Attractive. Overwhelmed. She's pretty much alone in the world other than having Walt."

"Uh-oh," Caleb said. "Sounds like a perfect candidate for the Benjamin-to-the-rescue club."

Tom grinned as Benjamin shot his younger brother a look of irritation. "It's not like that at all," he protested.

"She's only in town for a few days and she doesn't seem like the type who would want a man to run to her rescue. Is there anything new on the Jennifer Hightower disappearance?" he asked in an effort to change the subject.

"Not a damn thing," Tom replied.

As the three brothers ate their lunch, they discussed the latest disappearance of a young woman. Jennifer Hightower had gone to work at the convenience store on the edge of town as usual and had been scheduled to work until closing time at midnight. Her car had been left in the parking lot at the store, but she was nowhere to be found.

"The interviews with her friends have yielded nothing. We got nothing from her car. The surveillance tape from the store showed that she was alive and well at midnight when she closed up the place." Tom listed the facts one after another, his voice deep with frustration.

"She doesn't have a current boyfriend and her ex has a solid alibi," Caleb added. "It's like she vanished into thin air."

"Or somebody was waiting just outside for her," Tom said. "Too bad the convenience store doesn't have cameras outside."

"Have we decided that this case is connected to Brittany's?" Benjamin asked. It was the question that they'd all danced around for the past couple weeks.

Tom frowned, as if in pain. "There's no real evidence that they're connected. Jennifer doesn't look anything like Brittany. But the fact is we have two missing women.

I don't want to believe they're connected, but I guess we have to consider the possibility."

His words caused a knot of anxiety to form in Benjamin's chest. If the disappearances were connected, then that meant there was a possibility that somebody in town was kidnapping pretty young women. What he was doing to them was anybody's guess. Until a body was found it was impossible to speculate about what had become of the victims.

All he knew was that there was a new pretty young woman in town and the fear of an unknown darkness walking the streets of Black Rock.

Edie cursed beneath her breath as the lawn mower died for the fifth time in the past hour. She was exhausted, but wanted to get the lawn finished before calling it a day.

She'd been working at it for the past two hours. The problem was twofold: the lawn mower was an antique and the grass was so tall it kept gumming up the motor and conking it out.

Deciding to take a break, she eased down on the top stoop of the porch, thirsty but too tired to walk inside and get anything to drink.

She'd spoken with Poppy several times during the day. He wasn't a happy camper. "The nurse isn't pretty and I think she might be a vampire," he had groused. "Every time I turn around she's taking blood from me."

Edie had soothed him, grateful that the doctor had

agreed to run a battery of tests to see if Poppy's delusion was somehow a medical issue.

And if it wasn't? A little voice nagged in the back of her head. What did you do with somebody who thought they were seeing space aliens? Send them to therapy? Somehow she doubted that Black Rock had a resident therapist who might specialize in alien delusions.

All she could hope for was that Dr. Drake would find something with his tests that would account for the delusions and that whatever it was could be fixed with a pill.

All thoughts of her grandfather fled from her head as a familiar black pickup pulled into the driveway. Instantly her heart did an unexpected tap dance as Benjamin got out of the driver's seat.

Surely it was just because she'd been alone all day, she told herself. It had nothing to do with the fact that he was clad in a pair of killer jeans that hugged the length of his long legs and emphasized his lean abdomen. It had nothing to do with the glint in his eyes that perfectly matched the sexy, lazy grin that stretched his lips at the sight of her.

"Who's winning? You or the grass?" he asked as he drew closer.

"Definitely the grass," she replied as she got to her feet.

"It's too tall and the lawn mower is too old and I'm exhausted," she admitted. "What's going on? Did you find the person responsible for beating up Poppy?"

"I wish, unfortunately I don't have much to report."

He stepped closer to her, close enough that she could smell his cologne. "I went out by the cemetery and looked around. The only thing I found was what looks like a part of a key ring bob. It's engraved with the letter *A,* but I can't know if it had anything to do with the attack on Walt or not."

"Don't tell him what you found. He'll swear that the *A* stands for *alien,*" she said drily.

Benjamin laughed.

He had a nice laugh, deep and robust, like a man who enjoyed laughing.

"Actually, I just came from a visit with Walt."

"I spoke to him a couple hours ago and he wasn't too happy." She was overly conscious that the knees of her jeans were grass stained from weeding and she was wearing one of Poppy's oversize flannel shirts over her T-shirt. She didn't have on a stitch of makeup and the fact that it bothered her, bothered her.

"He's still not happy. He wanted me to stop by and pick up a pair of sleep pants that he says is more civilized than the ones at the hospital. He said they're in his top dresser drawer."

"Come on in and I'll get them for you." He walked too close behind her, not stopping in the living room but rather following her into Poppy's bedroom.

She hadn't been in this room for years and it was nothing like she remembered. When her grandmother had been alive the room had been a typical bedroom with the bed covered in a floral print spread and matching curtains at the window. The nightstands had held dainty little lamps and a trunk at the foot of the bed had contained a variety of sofa blankets that her grandmother had crocheted.

Now the bed was shoved against one wall and the nightstands and trunk were gone. A large desk took up much of the room. The top of the desk was cluttered with maps of the galaxy and of the town, notes jotted in Poppy's nearly illegible hand and an instant camera.

"It looks like headquarters for an alien hunter," Benjamin said as he picked up one of the maps of the stars.

"I'm really hoping the doctor will be able to find a medical reason for this craziness." Edie pulled open the top dresser drawer and found the pair of plaid sleep pants Walt had requested. She leaned her back against the dresser, every muscle in her body sore from her fight with the lawn mower.

"Too bad Walt didn't have this camera with him when the attack happened. He could have taken a picture of his assailant." Benjamin looked up from the desk. "You look tired. Why don't you let me finish up the lawn in the morning and you go take a shower and come with me for dinner at the café?"

"The grass isn't your responsibility. I couldn't ask you to finish," she replied.

"You didn't. I offered and you'd be a fool to turn me down," he said lightly.

"Okay, I'll let you finish the lawn in the morning, but I can just grab a sandwich here for dinner." She didn't want to think about going out to dinner with him. It would feel too much like a date and she had no intention of dating ever again.

"Edie." He took a step closer to her. "A nice hot meal will do you good. Besides, the special tonight is lasagna and it's terrific."

Lasagna definitely sounded yummy, and she was starving. She hesitated a beat and then nodded. "Okay, I'll meet you at the café," she finally said. At least that way she could eat and run.

He looked at his watch. "It's four-thirty now. Shall we meet in an hour?"

"Sounds perfect," she said as she followed him out of the bedroom. When they reached the front door, he turned back to look at her.

"You aren't going to stand me up, are you? I really hate when that happens."

She doubted that this man had ever been stood up in his life. "I'll be there," she replied.

The moment he left she raced up the stairs for a long hot shower, already regretting the agreement to meet him. She should have just stayed home and eaten a sandwich. There was something about Deputy Sheriff Benjamin Grayson that definitely put her on edge.

At five-twenty she drove slowly down Main Street looking for the café. She found it nestled between a taxidermy business and a veterinarian's office. As she pulled into a parking space down the street, a knot of nerves twisted in her stomach. *It's ridiculous to be nervous about a quick meal,* she told herself. She'd just eat fast and then get back to Poppy's house.

The evening had cooled a bit as the sun began to sink and she was grateful for the gold sweater she'd pulled on over a clean pair of jeans.

As she walked by the taxidermy store she shivered slightly at the animals in the window. A stuffed wolf looked ready to pounce on prey and a squirrel stood on its haunches with a nut between its paws. She'd never understood the desire to hang a deer head on a wall or stuff Fluffy to keep forever.

Dead was dead and no amount of stuffing and saving could change that. Her hand slid up to grip the charm around her neck. As always an edge of grief threatened to swell inside her, but she shoved it away, refusing to give it power.

Before she opened the café door she smelled the savory scents of frying onions and sweet tomato sauce and her stomach rumbled in response.

The minute she walked in the door, she saw Benjamin leaning against the long counter and talking to an attractive blonde waitress.

At the sound of the bell tinkling above the door with her entrance he turned and smiled at her, that sexy grin instantly heating places in Edie that hadn't been warm in a very long time.

He murmured something to the waitress and then approached Edie. "You came."

"I told you I would. I always do what I say I'm going to do. I'm hungry and too tired to fix something at home. This seemed like the most convenient thing to do." She was aware she sounded not only defensive, but more than a little bit cranky, as well.

It didn't seem to bother him. His eyes twinkling with good humor, he took her by the elbow and led her to an empty booth toward the back of the busy place.

As they made their way through the tables, he was greeted by everyone they passed. It was obvious Benjamin was well liked in the town he served. Not that she cared. He was just a hot, sexy blip in her radar who would be nothing but a distant memory weeks from now.

Once they were seated in the booth she picked up the menu, needing something to look at besides him. But the food listings were far less appealing than Benjamin.

She closed the menu and shoved it to one side. "Don't you have a wife or a girlfriend you should be having dinner with?"

"Don't have either," he replied and then grinned. "But thanks for being interested enough to ask."

"I'm not really interested. I was just making casual conversation." Awkward, she thought. This whole scene felt awkward. She should have made herself a sandwich at the house and called it a night. But the truth was the house had felt far too quiet without Poppy there.

"So, tell me something about Edie Burnett," he said.

"You know more about me than I'd intended for anyone to know," she replied darkly.

"All I really know is that you've had a run of bad

luck lately, but I'm sure there are far more interesting aspects to you."

She leaned back in the booth. "Why are you doing that?" she asked flatly.

He frowned in confusion. "Doing what?"

"Flirting with me." Although she wanted to look away she boldly held his gaze. "I don't know what you're looking for but you won't find it with me. I'm only in town for a short period and, besides, not only am I never going to date again, but I also intend to stay celibate for the rest of my life."

His eyebrows rose and then fell back into place. "A lot of men would consider that a real challenge," he said with that wicked glint in his eyes. The glint dimmed and he shook his head. "He must have hurt you very badly."

"It doesn't matter now, that's so in my past." She was grateful that the waitress appeared at that moment to take their orders.

They both ordered the lasagna special and when the waitress left, Edie took the reins of the conversation. "I pretty well spilled my life story to you when you pulled me over for speeding. Why don't you tell me something interesting about you?"

"Probably the most interesting thing about me is that I have three brothers and one sister and all of us went into law enforcement."

"Was your father a cop?" she asked.

"No, Dad was a genius when it came to buying and selling stocks. He worked the ranch and invested and did very well. When all of us kids got older, he and my mother traveled a lot."

"I know that one of your brothers is the sheriff. What about the others?" She began to relax a bit with the conversation steered away from her.

"Tom is the oldest and he's the sheriff. Then there's Jacob, who became an FBI agent. Caleb is a deputy like me and so was…is Brittany." He winced as he caught himself, but it was obvious to Edie that he wasn't expecting a happy ending where his sister was concerned.

"I'm sorry about your sister," Edie said softly.

"Yeah, so am I. And I was sorry to hear about your mother's death. My housekeeper told me that your mom was not only pretty but also a nice woman."

"She was the best," Edie said, then picked up her glass of water to take a sip and swallow her grief. "You've told me an interesting thing about your family. But tell me something about you personally." She was determined to keep the conversation on him, to focus on anything but herself and all the challenges she faced.

"Let's see." He leaned back against the booth and gave her that lazy smile that never failed to light a tiny fire inside her. "I like a horseback ride at sunset and big juicy steaks cooked outside. Green is my favorite color and I've got a dog named Tiny who thinks he's master of the world. I've never had a broken heart and I don't think I've ever broken one. How's that?" he said.

"Unbelievable," she replied. There was no way a man

who looked like Benjamin Grayson could have gone through his life so far and not broken a heart or two.

At that moment the waitress arrived with their orders and their conversation moved to more general things. He was pleasant to talk to and for a little while, she forgot all that was facing her. But she remained on edge, far too conscious of the allure of his flirtatious eyes and the warmth of his smile.

When her plate was empty she was ready to run. He offered to pay for the meal and after some argument, she accepted.

As they walked out of the café and into the deepening twilight of evening, he insisted he walk her to her car. "It's really not necessary," she protested. "I'm only parked down the street a little bit."

"I know, but it's a gentleman's duty to see a woman to her car," he replied lightly.

When they reached her vehicle, she pulled her keys from her purse, ready to bail and get away from Benjamin. "Thanks for dinner," she said as she unlocked her car door and then turned back to face him. "I appreciate everything you've done, but I can handle things now and you can get back to your own life."

"You aren't getting rid of me that easily," he replied. "I'll be over first thing in the morning to finish mowing the lawn. That was our deal."

She hesitated, not wanting to take anything more from him. He took a step closer to her. "Edie, you don't have to be in this all alone." He reached up and gently pushed one of her errant curls away from her forehead. "Walt is my friend and I'll do whatever I can to support you."

He dropped his hand back to his side but didn't move away from her. She felt as if she'd stopped breathing the moment he'd touched her and she forced herself to breathe now. "I appreciate that. Okay, then I guess I'll see you in the morning."

She'd let him finish the lawn and then she'd have nothing more to do with him. The last thing she needed in her life at the moment was another complication and Benjamin definitely felt as if he could be a big complication if she'd allow it.

For a moment he stared at her lips, as if he wanted to kiss her, and for that same amount of time she almost wished he would. Instead she jerked open her car door and wondered when she'd lost her mind.

"Edie, before you go take this." He pulled out a card from his pocket. "This has my personal cell phone number on it. Don't hesitate to use it if you need anything."

She took the card and dropped it into her purse and then slid in behind the steering wheel, eager to make her escape from this man who made her think about hot kisses and the sweet sensation of skin against skin.

She drove away without looking back, knowing that it was going to take her all night long to forget the feel of his warm fingers against her forehead, to get the very scent of him out of her head.

When she got back to Poppy's place, she called to check in on her grandfather, who was as cranky as she'd ever heard him, then she decided to vacuum and dust the living room.

She needed some sort of activity to occupy her and hopefully keep thoughts of Benjamin from her mind. But he was difficult to cast out of her head.

He was nice. He was definitely sexually drawn to her. She knew it by the look in his eyes, by the fact that he seemed to have trouble keeping his hands off her. Was he only being nice to her because he wanted to get her into bed?

Somehow he didn't strike her as that type and that was what worried her. She reluctantly had to admit that she liked him and that was on top of the wild physical attraction she felt toward him.

By the time she'd finished with the housework she was exhausted and she'd finally managed to banish thoughts of Benjamin from her mind.

She locked the front door and then headed upstairs for bed. Tomorrow she intended to call Poppy's doctor and get an update on the tests they had run on the old man. She prayed that Dr. Drake would be able to find an easy fix for Poppy's obsession and that Benjamin and his brothers would find and arrest whoever assaulted her grandfather.

Even though she was exhausted, once she was in bed her mind whirled with all the things waiting for her when she got back to Topeka. First and foremost on her list of things to do was find another job.

She'd loved managing the restaurant, but wasn't sure she wanted to go back into the same field. In truth she didn't know what she wanted to do with the rest of her life. A year ago she'd thought her future was all planned out. She'd marry Greg, be a wife and mother and decide on a career when their children went off to school.

Greg was on board right up until the time he disappeared from her life. Just like her father. She punched the pillow and closed her eyes, determined to get a good night's sleep without any more thoughts of betrayals from men.

I deserve it, a little voice whispered in her head. *I'm not good enough to be with anyone.* Emotion swelled up inside her but she steadfastly shoved it back down and squeezed her eyes more tightly closed.

She awoke suddenly, her heart pounding with unexpected adrenaline and her body tensed in a fight-or-flight response. Immediately she knew something had awakened her and as she remained frozen in place, she heard a faint noise coming from downstairs.

Somebody was in the house. The thought thundered in her brain. She knew she'd locked the front door before she'd come upstairs. But as she heard more noise she knew with certainty that somebody was there.

She swung her legs over the side of the bed and stood, then quietly crept to the top of the stairs. The noise was definitely coming from the direction of Poppy's bedroom.

Was it possible Poppy had somehow managed to talk the doctor into releasing him? She glanced at the clock on the nightstand, the luminous dial letting her know it was after one. Surely nobody would have released him in the middle of the night. It was more likely that Poppy had left on his own, slinking out like a thief in the dark. He could be so bullheaded at times.

She ran lightly down the stairs, aided by the bright moonlight that flooded in the living room windows. As she gazed toward Poppy's bedroom, she frowned in confusion. There were no lights on, but she saw the faint glow of a flashlight.

"Poppy?" The single word fell from her lips.

The flashlight whirled toward her, blinding her as it hit her eyes. She raised a hand in defense, but gasped as a big body collided with hers.

The force of the collision lifted her off her feet and as she fell, the back of her head slammed into the floor and she knew no more.

Chapter 4

Benjamin sat in his easy chair in the living room and channel-surfed. It was late and he should be in bed, but he was too restless to sleep and it was all thanks to Edie Burnett. Something about the woman had him twisted in knots.

He'd hated to tell her goodbye after dinner and was already eagerly anticipating going to Walt's in the morning to see her again.

It was a new feeling for him, this sweet anticipation, and one he'd never felt for a woman. It had heartbreak written all over it, but knowing that didn't seem to make him cautious.

He'd dated plenty over the past couple years but none of the women he'd seen had shot him full of the simmering excitement like Edie.

But she claimed she wanted nothing to do with men. Or sex. He'd never met a candidate less likely for celibacy. Those lips of hers were made for kissing and her curves were meant to be stroked and loved.

She definitely had some sharp edges that he guessed disillusionment had formed in her. It was that sharpness she used as a defense whenever he got too close.

As they'd eaten dinner, more than once when she got uncomfortable with the conversation, she'd reached up and touched the charm hanging on a gold chain around her neck. The charm was a pair of angel wings that he guessed was a symbol of the mother she'd lost.

He stroked Tiny's soft fur as he changed the channel for the hundredth time and realized that television in the middle of the night sucked. Tiny released a long-suffering sigh, probably wondering why they were in the chair and not in bed.

The ring of his cell phone jerked him upright. He fumbled in his pocket, pulled it out and answered.

"Benjamin, can you come over here?"

It took him a moment to recognize Edie's voice. She sounded strange, stressed to the max and needy. "What's wrong?"

A small burst of laughter escaped her. "I think the aliens have landed."

His stomach clenched with nervous energy. "I'll be right there." He didn't bother to ask her any more questions but instead hung up and was in his truck and headed to Walt's within minutes.

There was no question that something had happened,

something that had her spooked enough to call him. He tightened his hands on the steering wheel as he sped down the dark deserted streets.

At least he knew that whatever had happened, she was physically all right, at least enough to make the phone call to him. But emotionally she'd sounded fragile and he couldn't get to her fast enough.

When he pulled up the driveway, he saw her standing in the doorway. As he got out of his truck, she stepped on the porch. She was clad in a navy nightshirt that barely skimmed the tops of her thighs and her face was as pale as the moon overhead.

"What happened?" he asked as he reached the porch.

"Somebody was in the house, in Poppy's bedroom. I was in bed asleep and I woke up when I heard the noise. I thought it was Poppy, that maybe he'd left the hospital." She frowned and raised a hand to the back of her head.

He took her by the arm and led her into the house and to the sofa. "Are you hurt?" he asked, a new knot in his chest growing bigger. Her skin was cool and her arm trembled beneath his hand.

He wanted nothing more than to pull her against him and hold her tight until she was warm. But his first role was as a responding officer to a crime scene.

"I hit my head," she said. "He shoved past me and knocked me down and I hit my head on the floor."

He reached up and felt the back of her head and muttered a curse as he fingered the goose egg there. "We need to get you to the hospital and have that checked out," he said as she waved him away from her.

"It's fine. I'm fine. I was just out for a minute or two."

"Out? You mean like unconscious?"

She winced. "Stop shouting. I said I was okay."

Benjamin took a step backward, shocked as he realized he had been shouting and he'd never been a shouting kind of man in his life. He sat on the sofa next to her. "Tell me exactly what happened."

He listened and took notes as she told him about waking up and thinking Walt had come home. As she told him about seeing the intruder in Walt's bedroom and that person slamming into her, his blood went cold.

Thank God the intruder hadn't used a gun. When he thought of all the horrible scenarios that might have occurred, he went weak in the knees with relief.

"Did he take anything?" he asked.

"I don't know. I didn't go into the bedroom. When I came to, I just grabbed my purse from the kitchen counter and found your card."

He was grateful to see that some of the color was returning to her cheeks. "I'm going to call my brother and get him out here," he said. "And I'll see if I can rouse Dr. Drake to come over and examine you."

"That's really not necessary," she protested.

"I think it is. It's either see Dr. Drake here or head to the emergency room at the hospital. You were knocked unconscious. You need to be checked out."

She managed to glare at him. "You sound pretty bossy."

"At the moment I'm feeling pretty bossy." As she leaned her head back and closed her eyes, he made his phone calls. When he was finished she raised her head once again to look at him.

"Maybe it was somebody who heard through the grapevine that Poppy was in the hospital and decided to take advantage of the situation by robbing the place," she said. "My car is in the garage. I don't think the person knew I was here."

"That's possible," he agreed. "I'm going to check out Walt's bedroom. I'll be right back."

"I'll go with you." She jumped up off the sofa and a flash of pain momentarily twisted her features.

"Why don't you sit and relax? It's obvious you have a headache." Once again he fought the impulse to take her into his arms.

"I'd feel better staying with you."

Her words let him know just how spooked she still was. She followed close behind him and together they went into Walt's room. "Don't touch anything," he cautioned as he used his elbow to turn on the light in the room.

"Don't worry," she said drily.

Two things struck Benjamin as he looked around the room. The first was that all the windows were still intact and locked, indicating the point of entry had been someplace else in the house. The second was that it was obvious somebody had been in the room. The papers that had been on top of the desk were now strewn across the floor. Drawers hung open with clothes spilling out and boxes had been pulled off the shelves in the closet.

"If they were looking for something of value, they came to the wrong house," Edie said.

"Can you tell if anything is missing?" he asked.

He watched as she gazed around the room and frowned. "Nothing that I can see. Wait…remember the camera that was on the desk? I don't see it anywhere now."

He walked around the desk, checking the floor to see if perhaps the camera had fallen off, but it was nowhere to be seen.

"What on earth has Poppy gotten himself involved in?" Edie asked softly.

"I don't know, but somehow we're going to figure it out," he replied.

At that moment Tom arrived at the scene, followed closely by Dr. Drake. As the doctor examined Edie, Tom and Benjamin got to work processing the scene.

The entry point was the front door, which held an old lock that had been jimmied open. Whoever had come in had apparently gone directly to Walt's bedroom, for there was no indication that anything else had been disturbed.

Dr. Drake pronounced that Edie probably had a mild concussion and would be fine and then he left. By that time Tom had dusted the front door for prints and Benjamin had dusted the bedroom. Benjamin had little hope of lifting anything. Whoever had broken in was probably smart enough to wear gloves.

Edie had nothing to offer as far as what the person had looked like. It had been dark and everything had happened too fast. All she could be sure of was that he'd been big and dark and had hit her like an NFL tackle.

It was after three when they had done all they could for the night and Tom left. Edie was curled up in one corner of the sofa, looking small and exhausted.

Benjamin sat next to her. "How's your head?"

"Better than it was. At least now it's down to a three-piece band instead of a full percussion orchestra." She released a weary sigh.

"You need to get a new lock on the front door. It probably wouldn't hurt to put a new one on the back door, as well. I'll get somebody to take care of it first thing in the morning."

"Thank you," she replied. "I have to confess, I'm a little bit nervous about staying here all alone for the rest of the night without the locks fixed."

He knew better than to think she was issuing an invitation for him to spend the night with her, but he couldn't stop the slight flush of heat that filled him at the very thought.

"I guess you have two options," he said, pleased that his voice sounded normal. "I can either take you to a motel for the rest of the night or I could stay here until morning."

She shot him a narrowed glance and he did everything possible to keep his features without any expression.

The last thing he wanted her to think was that he was somehow taking advantage of the situation.

Releasing another deep sigh, she sat up straighter. "I guess it would be stupid to go to a motel at this time of the night. I'll get you some blankets and a pillow so you can bunk here on the sofa."

"Or, just for your information, I've been told I make a terrific snuggle buddy."

"Deputy Grayson, surely *snuggle buddy* isn't in your job description," she said as she rose to her feet.

"It could be," he replied as he also stood.

"That's so not happening," she said. "But I might share a little conversation with you over a cup of tea before I turn in."

"Sounds like a plan," he agreed easily. As he followed her into the kitchen, he admitted that he'd much prefer a place in her bed, but as she'd reminded him moments before—that was so not happening tonight.

The hot tea didn't quite banish the chill that had taken hold of Edie since the moment she'd come to on the living-room floor.

"Talk to me, Benjamin, tell me more about the ranch where you live," she said, needing something, anything to take her mind off the fact that somebody had been in the house while she'd been asleep and vulnerable.

What might have happened if she hadn't awakened when she did? Would the intruder have eventually crept up the stairs and found her? Would a simply robbery have escalated to something worse—her rape? Her murder?

As Benjamin began to talk about his life at the ranch, his eyes took on the sparkle of a man who loved that life and his deep voice filled with a vibrancy that was vastly appealing.

As he talked of cattle and horses and his daily routine when at home, she felt herself begin to finally relax. There was something solid about Benjamin and the life he led, something that reminded her of all the hopes she'd once possessed, all the dreams she'd once had for herself.

She'd once wanted the kind of life he was describing, one of normal routine and peace, filled with the love of family and the kind of happiness that came from knowing where you belonged.

It had been a long time since she'd felt as if she belonged anywhere. Looking back now, she recognized that there had always been a little part of her that had suspected Greg wasn't the man for her. But she'd been desperate to be loved, tired of being alone and had clung to him despite her reservations.

Greg hadn't been her first mistake. Before him had been Charles, a man she'd dated for almost a year, a man who hadn't known the meaning of fidelity. Loving stupid, that was what she was good at, and it was better to never love again than continue making the same mistakes.

Her head began to pound again as if in protest of her thoughts and exhaustion slammed into her with a force that made her long for the comfort of bed. "I've got to go to bed," she said as she pushed back from the kitchen table. "The extra blankets are upstairs in the closet. I'll just get what you need for the sofa."

He got up, as well. "I'll follow you so you don't have to make an extra trip down the stairs."

"Thanks," she replied and wondered if he was always so nice. She was far too conscious of him behind her as she climbed the stairs.

"Blankets in there?" He pointed ahead of them to the hall closet. "I'll take care of myself," he continued as she nodded. "Let's get you tucked into bed."

She walked to her bedroom doorway and then turned to face him. "Thank you, Benjamin, for agreeing to stay here for whatever is left of the night. I'll be fine once the new locks are installed."

"It's not a problem." He took a step closer to her, so close she could smell the scent of him, feel the heat that radiated from his body. "You had a scare and I'm glad to do whatever I can to make you feel safe."

She felt wonderfully safe and intensely in danger with him standing so close to her. "I guess I'll say goodnight."

"Wait, there's just one thing I've been wanting to do all night." He reached out and pulled her against him, close enough that she could feel his heartbeat beneath the solid wall of his chest.

She held herself stiffly but as his hand slid up and down her back as if to comfort, she allowed herself to relax against him. She hadn't realized just how badly she'd needed a hug until now.

The feel of him against her, so warm, so strong, finally banished the last of the chill that had resided in her since the moment she'd awakened and realized somebody was in the house.

Moments passed and the slide of his hand over her back slowed and instead of being comforted, Edie felt a new tension building between them.

She raised her head to look at him and saw the flames that filled his eyes. Instantly she knew that she should step out of his arms, gain some distance from him.

She did neither.

As his mouth descended toward hers, she opened her lips to welcome the kiss, telling herself she could always justify the madness by claiming brain numbness from her fall.

His mouth plied hers with a welcome heat, his tongue touching hers as he tightened his arms around her. *Falling,* she felt herself falling into him, consumed by him as all other thoughts fled her mind.

She tasted his desire for her, a desire tempered with a tenderness that threatened to be her undoing, and that was ultimately what made her halt the kiss.

A small groan escaped him as he dropped his arms from around her and took a step back. "Are you sure about this celibacy thing?" he asked with a teasing grin.

"One little kiss isn't about to change my mind," she replied. "Good night, Benjamin." She escaped into the bedroom and closed the door behind her, needing to gain some distance from him.

She fell into bed, exhausted by the events of the night, but sleep refused to come easily. The kiss. It was that kiss that haunted her. And the man.

Benjamin Grayson was like no man she'd ever known before and he scared her. She needed to keep her distance from him until she left Black Rock to return home.

But how soon could she get back home? With Poppy getting beaten up and the break-in tonight, how could she possibly consider leaving? She wasn't sure what worried her more, the mess of Poppy or the insane attraction she felt for Benjamin.

She fell asleep with the taste of him on her lips and awakened with the sun streaming through her window and the sound of the lawn mower growling from the front yard.

By the time she'd showered and dressed for the day, the noise outside had stopped. She found Benjamin in the kitchen, seated at the table and sipping a cup of coffee. The very sight of him brought back the memory of the devastating kiss and an irritation surged up inside her.

"Shouldn't you be at work chasing bad guys?" she asked sharply. "This town is obviously infested with them."

One of his dark eyebrows rose. "Sounds like somebody got up on the wrong side of the bed." A blush warmed her cheeks as she headed for the coffee. "I contacted Ed Burell, the local locksmith. He'll be here in the next half hour or so to take care of changing the locks."

"Thanks, I appreciate your help," she said as she joined him at the table. It was impossible to be cranky with him when he was going out of his way to make her life easier.

"My brother Caleb is already out interviewing the neighbors to see if they saw anyone or anything suspicious last night. Tom has been talking to some of the high-school kids to see if they know anything about Walt's attack and I've already alerted everyone in town who processes film to give me a call if somebody brings in an instant camera. There's not much else that can be done at the moment."

"I didn't mean to sound like I thought you weren't doing your job," she replied. "I just wish we could figure out what's going on."

"We will." There was a fierce determination in his voice. "Sooner or later the person who attacked Walt will be caught and charged with the crime. This is a small town and eventually somebody will say something and we'll have our man."

"And hopefully the doctor will tell me all Poppy needs is a pill to fix him right up and I can get back home."

"Now, I've got to admit I'm not in any hurry to see you go." He stood and carried his cup to the sink. "But speaking of going, I need to get out of here." He turned back to face her. "Do you want me to wait with you until the locksmith arrives?"

"No, I'll be fine," she assured him. "I do appreciate everything you've done. Just keep me informed about the investigations and that's all I really need from you." It was an obvious dismissal. "An occasional check-in phone call would be great."

Once again that well-shaped dark brow rose and a twinkle filled his eyes. "That kiss was either very, very bad or very, very good."

The familiar warmth of a blush heated her cheeks. "That kiss was stupid, the result of a head injury that didn't have me thinking clearly."

He laughed. "If that's what you need to tell yourself to get through the day, then so be it. I'm sure I'll talk to you later."

She remained seated at the table as he left the house, trying to ignore the slow burn that he created inside her. Okay, she could admit that she was intensely physically attracted to him, but the kiss they had shared was the beginning and the end of acting on that attraction.

She'd only been seated at the table for about ten minutes when Ed Burell arrived to change the locks on the doors. He left after handing her the new keys.

Edie left soon after that, deciding a visit to Poppy was in order. As she drove down Main Street, she found herself looking at the various businesses.

There was a cute little dress boutique, the Canyon Pizzeria, the café and dozens of other businesses. Unlike many small Kansas towns that had fallen on hard times,

Black Rock seemed to be thriving despite the current economic climate.

Edie parked on the street next to the small hospital. She walked inside and headed to the second floor where Poppy's room was located. When she entered his room, she was surprised to see him dressed and seated on the edge of his bed. A plump nurse with a pretty smile greeted her.

"I just tried to call you," Poppy said. "I can go home. Fit as a fiddle, that's what I am, other than my black eye and cracked ribs. Dr. Drake gave me all kinds of tests and says he wishes he was as healthy as I am."

Edie looked at the nurse, who nodded in affirmation. "He's good to go," she replied. "Dr. Drake should be in any moment if you have any questions."

Moments later a talk with the doctor in the hallway let Edie know he'd found no medical reason for her grandfather's delusion. There was nothing more he could do but release him.

A half hour later they were back home. As Walt prepared lunch, Edie sat at the table and listened to him regaling his hospital adventure to her.

She tried not to be depressed as she realized she was no closer to solving the problem of Poppy than she'd been before his attack. Granted, somebody had beaten up the old man, but it definitely hadn't been a space alien.

As they ate she brought him up-to-date on the break-in and the new locks on the doors. When she told him that the only thing that had been missing was his camera, he blew a gasket.

"The bastards knew I had pictures of them. The night before you arrived here." He got up from the table with jerky movements that spoke of his irritation. "I was going to take that camera down to Burt Smith's discount store to get the pictures developed."

"Poppy, you have to get this idea of aliens out of your head," Edie exclaimed.

"Out of my head? I'm not about to get those bastards out of my head. Tonight I'm going hunting again and this time I'm going to take my gun."

Edie stared at him appalled. Just what Black Rock needed, a crazy man with a gun out in the middle of the night.

Chapter 5

It was just before midnight when Edie and her grandfather left his house. Edie knew it was madness but at least she'd managed to talk Poppy into leaving his gun at home. The good people of Black Rock should give her an award.

"Where are we headed?" she asked once they were in the car and pulling out of the driveway.

"Go south on Main Street, I'll tell you where to turn off when we get there," he replied. He was clad all in black, like a ninja warrior ready for battle.

"Are we going back to the cemetery?"

"Nah, lately on Friday nights they've been in Devon Moreland's clearing," he replied.

Not for the first time since agreeing to this madness, Edie's thoughts turned to Benjamin.

Edie had considered calling Benjamin to ask him to come over and help her change Poppy's mind about going out tonight, but after some thought she'd decided against it.

What worried her was the idea that perhaps she wanted to call Benjamin not because she needed his help with Poppy, but just because she wanted to see him again.

Earlier she'd listened to Poppy talk about his time in the hospital and while he'd napped she'd watched television, but no matter how she tried to keep her mind occupied, thoughts of Benjamin and the kiss they'd shared kept intruding.

He'd kissed her as if he'd meant it, as if it were a prelude to something hot and wild, yet something tender and enduring. She didn't want to believe in the promise of his kiss and if what he'd told her about himself was right, she didn't want to be the first woman in his life to break his heart.

And she would break his heart if he tried to pursue anything with her. Even if he thought he might be the right man for her, she definitely knew she was the wrong woman for him.

At this time of the night the streets were dark and deserted. Edie drove slowly, wishing they were back at the house and not on some crazy hunt for aliens.

"This is the kind of night they like," Poppy said, breaking the silence. He leaned forward to look up at the sky through the windshield. "See them clouds chasing across the moon? They like cloudy nights. Turn left up ahead."

She made the turn and tried not to feel as if she were indulging Poppy's fantasy. They both should be home in bed, but she was hoping that she would see whatever it was that made the old man insist there were aliens in town. Then maybe she'd be able to make him understand that he'd been mistaken.

"How are you doing with that boyfriend of yours?" Poppy asked.

Edie tightened her hands on the steering wheel. "We broke up," she said, pleased that her voice remained neutral.

"Turn left here," he said. "So, does that mean you have a new beau?"

"At the moment I'm footloose and fancy-free, and that's just the way I want it," she replied as she focused on the narrow road they traveled.

"Turn right up ahead," Poppy said.

She felt as if they'd entered a forest. Trees crowded together so closely that the moonlight was obscured overhead. "You can park right up there under that oak tree and we'll walk the rest of the way."

"How did you find this place?" Edie asked as she parked her car and shut off the engine.

"I didn't find it, the aliens did and I found them. It took me a couple months to figure out their routine. Some nights they're in the cemetery and then some nights they're out here." He grabbed the flashlight he'd brought with him and opened his car door. "Come on,

I've got a perfect hiding place where you'll be able to see them."

Edie left the car and followed close behind Poppy as he took off walking through the thick woods, his flashlight beam bouncing in the darkness with each step he took.

No wonder Poppy was in such good physical shape, she thought. On the nights he went alien hunting he must walk miles. They didn't go far before he gestured her down behind a large bush.

"See that clearing?" He pointed the flashlight beam forward to reveal a small break in the woods. "That's where I've seen one of them several times before." He shut off the flashlight and sat in the grass, indicating that she should do the same. "Now we wait and see if one of the bastards show up tonight."

Edie settled in next to Poppy and for the next few minutes the only sounds were those of a soft breeze stirring the leaves overhead and insects buzzing and clicking their night songs.

"You know you won't find a better man than Benjamin," Poppy whispered, breaking the silence.

Startled by his words, she tried to see his face in the darkness. "I'm really not looking for a man, Poppy."

"I'm just saying. Most of the women in town seem to find him attractive, but he's not a trifling man. Out of all the Grayson men he's always been my favorite. Tom is a take-charge kind of guy and Caleb is impulsive and easy to rile. Jacob was always a loner but Benjamin is solid as the earth and has a good heart."

As Poppy continued to extol Benjamin's virtues, all Edie could think about was the dark chocolate color of his eyes as they filled with desire and that crazy hot kiss they had shared.

"I keep telling him he should forget his deputy job and work full-time at the ranch. That's what he loves, working with the animals and the land."

Edie remembered the passion that had filled his voice when he'd talked about the ranch. "If that's what he loves to do then why isn't he doing it full-time?"

"Don't know. I can't ever get a solid answer from him."

They both fell silent once again. The minutes ticked by in agonizing slowness. After half an hour of sitting, the ground seemed to grow harder beneath Edie and sleepiness began to creep in.

They both should be home asleep, not sitting outside in the brisk autumn night air waiting for aliens to appear. She should especially not be out here thinking about Benjamin Grayson, warmed by the memory of the kiss they had shared.

"Poppy, let's go home," she finally said when another fifteen minutes or so had passed. "It's really late and I'm tired."

He sighed, obviously disappointed. "I wanted you to see one of the aliens. I want you to know that I'm not crazy. I know everyone in town thinks I've done gone around the bend, but I'm not nuts."

"Poppy, I don't think you're nuts," she protested softly.

"You're just like your mama, Edie girl. You have her good heart," he replied, a smile obvious in his voice. "I've missed you, Edie. I've missed your phone calls. You're the only family I've got left."

Edie's "good" heart squeezed tight in her chest. Was it possible this whole alien thing was nothing more than a manifestation of Walt's loneliness?

"I've missed you, too, Poppy. And I promise I'm going to be better about keeping in touch with you," she replied.

Before he could answer, the sound of a low motor filled the air. "Here they come," Poppy exclaimed.

Edie peeked through the brush and in the distance saw a small lit vehicle approaching the clearing. It took her only an instant to realize it was an off-road ATV, but with the lights radiating out from it, she could easily see how a confused old man might think it was some kind of a space terrain vehicle.

"Poppy, keep down and keep quiet," she said as the vehicle came to a stop. Her heart slammed against her chest in a frantic tattoo. What would somebody be doing on an ATV in the middle of the woods at this time of night? Certainly nothing good, she thought.

The ATV shut off and Edie gripped Poppy's arm tightly, hoping and praying the old man didn't suddenly jump up to confront the driver.

Her curiosity turned to fear when the lone man stepped off the ATV and she realized he wore some sort of full hazmat suit. No wonder Poppy had thought the aliens had landed.

With the moonlight playing on the silver suit and reflecting off the mirrorlike face of the helmet, the man looked not only otherworldly but also ominous. What on earth was going on?

He carried with him a small spade and some sort of bag that held an eerie yellow-green glow. As Edie and Poppy watched, the man quickly dug a hole and dropped the bag inside.

"I'll bet that's the one who beat me." Poppy's voice was far too loud for the silence in the clearing. The man's head lifted as Edie held her breath and squeezed Poppy's arm even harder.

The man raised a high-beam flashlight and began to shine it in their direction as he pulled a gun with his other hand. Edie gasped as the light found them.

"Poppy, run," she said urgently. She got to her feet and yanked up the old man by his arm.

At the same time she heard the crash of brush ahead and knew the man was coming after them. A scream released from her as the crack of a gun splintered the air.

Thankfully Poppy was spry and seemed to know the woods. They held hands and ran as fast as their legs would take them. In the distance she heard the whine of the ATV and knew their pursuer had stopped his foot chase but intended to continue on the ATV.

The lights from the all-terrain vehicle bounced off the trees as the engine whined and crashed through the brush. With each step she took, Edie feared a bullet in her back.

Poppy's beating had obviously been some sort of warning, but the fact that the man had shot a gun at them let her know he wasn't warning anymore.

She nearly sobbed in relief as they made it back to her car. Poppy fell into the passenger seat while she threw herself in behind the steering wheel and punched the key into the ignition. As the engine roared to life she slammed the gear shift into Reverse.

The tires spun as she wheeled the car around for a quick escape. At the same time the ATV burst through the trees just behind them. Edie screamed and Poppy cursed as their back windshield shattered.

"Drive, girl!" Poppy yelled. "Put the pedal to the metal!"

Edie did just that, flooring the gas pedal and praying that the old clunker didn't pick this particular time to conk out. She flew down the road, barely making the turn that would eventually lead them back into the heart of the town.

"Yee-haw," Poppy yelled. "We lost him."

Edie looked in her rearview mirror and released a shuddering sigh of relief, but there was no relief from the fear that still torched through her. There was only one man she wanted to see, one man who could make her feel safe in what had become a crazy world.

"Tell me how to get to Benjamin's," she said. She wasn't sure what bothered her more, the fact that some crazy man in a hazmat suit had tried to kill them or her desperate need to be with a man she knew she shouldn't want.

* * *

He was dreaming about her. Somewhere in the back of his sleep-addled mind Benjamin knew it was a dream and that he didn't want to ever wake up.

Edie was in his arms, her green eyes glowing with smoky desire. His head filled with the scent of her, that slightly wild spicy fragrance that drove him half-wild.

Her skin was warm and silky against his and he wanted to take her, possess her in a way he'd never possessed another woman.

He was just about to do that when a loud banging broke the dream. Tiny began to bark and jumped off the foot of his bed and raced out of the room.

As the last vestige of the dream fell away, Benjamin leaped out of bed and grabbed the jeans he'd shucked off before going to sleep. As he yanked them on, the knocking at the front door continued. He grabbed his gun from the nightstand and then hurried out of the bedroom and down the hallway, turning on lights as he went.

What the hell? As he pulled open the door Edie and Walt tumbled inside. "He tried to kill us!" Walt exclaimed as Tiny's barks grew sharper. "The bastard shot out the back window of Edie's car."

Benjamin had no idea what was going on or what had happened, but Walt's words ripped a surge of unexpected protectiveness through him as he looked at Edie.

Her eyes were wide, her face pale and he quickly placed his hands on her shoulders and then ran them down her arms, ending with her trembling hands in his. "Are you all right?"

She gave a curt nod of her head. "I'm okay, and it wasn't a space alien, but it was a man in a hazmat suit on an ATV."

"A hazmat suit?" Walt looked as bewildered as Benjamin felt at the moment.

"Come on, let's all go into the kitchen and you can tell me what's going on." Reluctantly Benjamin released Edie's hands and they headed toward the kitchen.

Once there Benjamin gestured them into chairs at the table and as he sat, Tiny curled up at his feet, obviously exhausted by his earlier frantic barking. "Now, start at the beginning and tell me exactly what happened."

As Edie told him the events of the night, a hard knot of tension formed in his chest, first that she and Walt would be foolish enough to venture out in the middle of the night and second because something terrible was obviously going on under the cover of night in the small town he loved.

"Where exactly did this happen?" he asked.

"That little clearing on Devon Moreland's land," Walt said with a frown. "So, they aren't space men?" He looked at Edie and for a moment appeared older than his years.

She reached out and covered the old man's hand with one of hers. "No, Poppy. The man in the woods was definitely human."

Walt frowned and shook his head. "I feel like such a damned old fool."

"He looked like a spaceman. Anyone might have made the same mistake," Edie said gently and then looked at Benjamin. "He was burying something in the clearing. When he saw us, he pulled a gun and shot at us, then chased us on his ATV. He stopped chasing us when we hit Main Street."

"But not before he blew out the back window of her car," Walt added.

"I don't suppose there's any way you could make an identification?" Benjamin asked, although he knew the answer even before she shook her head.

"Impossible. With that suit on I couldn't even swear that it was definitely a man and not a woman," she replied.

Benjamin scooted back his chair from the table. "I don't want you two going home tonight. Why don't I get you settled in here and we'll talk more in the morning."

"I am tired," Walt agreed as he also got up from the table. "I don't like putting you out, but I have to confess I'd feel more comfortable at your place tonight."

"I'll just wait here while you get him settled in," Edie said.

It took only a few minutes for Benjamin to make Walt comfortable in one of the guest bedrooms. As he headed back into the kitchen, his head reeled with all the information he'd heard. The idea of how close Edie and Walt had come to disaster horrified him.

He found her still in the chair at the table with Tiny

in her lap. "What a sweet baby," she said as she stroked Tiny's dark fur.

"Don't let him fool you. Beneath that goofy grin of his is a mutt determined to rule the world." He was glad to see that she looked better than when she and Walt had initially flown through his front door.

"I hate to even ask this, but do you think you could take me back to where you and Walt were tonight? It's been years since I've been anywhere near Devon Moreland's property."

"I think so," she replied.

"I need to make some calls, get things lined up and then we'll head out." Although the last thing he wanted was to drag her out of the house once again, he needed her to show him exactly where all this had gone down.

He wasn't worried about Walt somehow sneaking out again. As he prepared to leave he checked on the old man, who was snoring up a storm. Besides, if he awakened, the ranch was too far out of town for him to try to walk anywhere.

The first thing he did was call Tom and fill him in on what had occurred then made arrangements to meet both Tom and Caleb at the sheriff's office in thirty minutes.

He pulled on a shirt and a jacket, checked on Walt one last time and then he and Edie got into his truck to make the drive back into town.

"I'm sorry you got involved in all this," he said.

"Me, too. Although I'm more than a little curious to

see what *all this* is," she admitted. "That scene in the woods tonight felt like something out of a science fiction movie."

"You and Walt could have been killed," he said with a touch of censure.

"I know, we shouldn't have been out there, but Poppy's original plan was to take his gun and go alien hunting. I got him to agree to leave his gun at home by going with him."

Benjamin fought a shudder as he thought of the old man armed and running amok in the darkness. "I guess I should thank God for small favors."

She released a sigh. "I was hoping that I would see something that had a logical explanation, something that would make me able to convince him there were no aliens in town."

He glanced at her and then back at the road. "I don't want you out again that late at night."

"Don't worry. I can say for sure that tonight was the first and the last of my alien hunting," she replied drily.

"I'd also like for you and Walt to stay at the ranch until we figure out what's going on," he added.

"Surely that isn't necessary," she protested.

"I think it is," he replied smoothly but firmly. "Those were real bullets that were fired at you tonight. We have to assume that the break-in at Walt's is related, and that means he knows who you are and where you live. You saw him doing something he obviously didn't want anyone to see and now he'll see you as a real threat."

As a deputy sheriff he wanted her at his place because he thought it was the best place for her to be. But his desire to have her stay at the ranch transcended his role as a deputy.

As a man he needed to protect what was his and even though he'd only known her for a couple days, somehow in that span, he recognized that he'd claimed her as his own.

He glanced at her again and saw the frown that whipped across her features. She sighed with weary resignation. "I guess I'd be a fool not to stay here."

At that moment they pulled up in front of the sheriff's office where Tom's car was already parked. "I sent Caleb over to the fire department to pick us up a couple suits," Tom said after he'd greeted them. "I figure if the perp felt the need to wear a hazmat suit when he was disposing of whatever he had, it's best if we have them on when we dig it up."

"Good idea," Benjamin replied with a reassuring glance at Edie. She offered him a weak smile and at that moment Caleb arrived and they all headed to the area where Edie and Walt had encountered the man.

Tom and Caleb rode together in Tom's car and followed Benjamin and Edie. "It sounds like Walt stumbled on some sort of illegal dumping," he said as they left Main Street.

"At least we've solved the mystery of the space aliens and I know Poppy isn't crazy." She reached out and directed the heater vent to blow on her face.

"Cold?"

"Just chilled by everything that's happened. Turn left ahead."

He made the turn and checked his rearview mirror to see his brother's car right behind his. "I suppose with everything that's happened lately now wouldn't be a good time to ask you if you've considered moving to Black Rock."

"Why would I consider doing that?" she countered.

So I'd have the opportunity to see you every day of my life. The words played in his head but thankfully didn't make it to his lips. "I know you're going to be looking for a new job and a new place to live. I'm sure Walt would love having you here in town."

"Maybe, but that's not in my plans. We parked up there next to that tree." She pointed ahead.

Benjamin pulled to a halt and cursed himself for being a fool. He seemed to be suffering his first major crush on a woman and other than her response to his kiss, she appeared fairly oblivious to his charms.

He only hoped that this crazy, giddy feeling he got whenever he was around her would fade as he got to know her better.

They all departed their vehicles and it was quickly decided that Benjamin and Tom would don the hazmat suits and go into the clearing while Caleb stayed with Edie.

The minute Benjamin was suited up all thoughts of romance and Edie fled from his mind. This was business and the fact that he and his brother wore hazmat suits meant it was serious business.

Together he and Tom made their way slowly into the clearing, their high-powered flashlight beams leading the way. The woods were still, as if any creatures had long left the area and were afraid to return.

Benjamin had his gun in hand, although he didn't anticipate any trouble. Whoever had taken a couple shots at Walt and Edie from this clearing would be long gone.

Tom carried a metal container specifically designed to transport anything toxic they might find and in his other hand he carried a shovel. Edie had indicated that the person had buried something in a bag, so they weren't looking for some kind of dump of liquid chemicals.

Once they reached the clearing, Tom set down the container and shovel and shone his flashlight on the ground. Benjamin did the same, seeking evidence of a burial site.

It didn't take them long to find not one, but three different areas where it looked as if the ground had recently been disturbed.

Tom picked up his shovel and approached one of the areas. As Benjamin kept his light focused on the ground, Tom began to dig.

He'd removed only three shovels of dirt when Benjamin saw the glow Edie had told him about, a faint yellowish-green glow that definitely looked otherworldly.

He exchanged a worried glance with Tom. What in the hell was going on out here? What on earth could be the source of the weird glow?

His chest tightened with tension as dozens of crazy speculations raced through his head. There were no factories in town, no businesses that might generate any form of glowing toxic waste.

Another swipe with the shovel exposed a white plastic shopping bag with the name of the local grocer printed on the side. It was loosely tied at the top and together the two brothers crouched down to get a closer look.

It was obvious that the glow was coming from whatever was inside the bag. With a dry throat, Benjamin leaned over and untied the bag. As he looked inside a gasp of horror spilled out of him.

An arm.

An arm complete with a hand.

A tattoo of a snake decorated the skin just above the wrist, a tattoo Benjamin immediately recognized. The arm belonged to Jim Taylor, a seventy-eight-year-old man who had finally lost his battle with cancer two weeks ago, a man who had been buried in the cemetery about ten days earlier.

Chapter 6

"Walt Tolliver, what in blazes are you doing in my kitchen?"

The strident female voice pulled Edie abruptly from sleep. She remained buried beneath the blankets, reluctant to rise since she'd only gone to bed a couple hours before. A glance at the window let her know the sun was just beginning to break over the horizon.

"What do you think I'm doing? I'm looking to make myself some breakfast," Walt replied.

As their voices grew softer, Edie closed her eyes once again, but sleep refused to immediately return. It had been after three when Caleb had finally driven her back to the ranch. Benjamin and Tom had remained in the woods and all Caleb would tell her was that the clearing was officially an active crime scene.

She had no idea what kind of crime had occurred there, but the thought that she'd seen part of it in progress chilled her to the bone.

She must have fallen asleep again, for when she next opened her eyes, the sun was shining fully into the room and she felt rested.

Sitting up, she looked around the room where she had slept. Caleb had told her that Benjamin wanted her in the guest room with the yellow bedspread. It was on the opposite side of the house from the bedroom where Walt had slept and across the hall from the master bedroom.

She knew it was the master bedroom because when she'd been looking for her room she'd gone into it first. The king-size bed looked as if somebody had jumped up in a hurry, the blankets and sheets tossed carelessly aside. The entire room had smelled of him and for just a minute as she'd gazed at the bed, she'd wanted to crawl into it and be enveloped by his scent.

The room where she'd slept was pleasant enough, with buttercup walls and yellow gingham curtains at the window. She had no idea what to expect from the day, but was eager to hear from Benjamin about exactly what they had discovered in the clearing.

She got up and went into the bathroom across the hall for a quick shower. As she put on the same clothes, she made a mental note that if they were going to stay here another night she needed to go to Poppy's place and pick up some clothes for both of them.

She left the bathroom and headed down the hallway

and into the living room, where she looked around, interested in the place Benjamin called home.

The requisite flat-screen television hung above the stone fireplace and the sofa was a brown and black pattern. She knew instinctively that the black recliner would be Benjamin's seating of choice. She could easily imagine him there, his long legs stretched out before him and Tiny on his lap.

Thinking about the dog, she wondered where he was this morning. When she entered the kitchen she got her answer. Poppy sat at the table eating what smelled like a freshly baked blueberry muffin and Tiny sat at his feet, obviously waiting for any crumb that might fall to the floor.

The dog wagged his tail at the sight of her and at the same time a gray-haired older woman who stood at the stove turned and smiled. "There she is," she exclaimed.

She bustled to Edie's side and led her to a chair at the table. "I'm Margaret, honey, not that your grandfather would think of making an introduction."

"Hell's bells, Margaret, you didn't give me a chance to introduce you," Walt grumbled. "She can talk a body to death, that one can," he said to Edie, but he had a distinct sparkle in his eyes.

"Don't listen to him," Margaret said. "How about I whip you up some breakfast? Maybe some pancakes or eggs and toast?"

"If Edie wants breakfast I'll be more than happy to fix her something," Walt said as he began to rise.

"This is my kitchen," Margaret said in a huff. "I'll do the cooking around here."

"Poppy, finish your muffin, and thank you, Margaret, but I'm really not hungry. However, a cup of coffee would be great," Edie said.

Margaret got her the coffee and then sat at the table across from her. "You look just like your mama, God rest her soul," she said. "A sweet girl she was and I was sorry to hear about her death."

"Thanks," Edie replied. "Is Benjamin home?"

"No. That poor boy isn't home yet. Walt told me some of what happened last night." She cast the old man a begrudging glance. "Guess he's not as crazy as we all thought he was."

"Just stupid, that's what I was," Poppy exclaimed. "Thinking a hazmat suit was some sort of a space suit."

"It's a mistake anyone could make," Margaret said gruffly as a faint pink stained her cheeks. Poppy looked at her with surprise and then down at his muffin as a slight blush colored his cheeks, as well.

Edie sensed a little attraction in the air between the two. Good, she thought. If Poppy had a woman friend to keep him company, then Edie wouldn't feel so bad about eventually going home.

And shouldn't she be thinking about going home? Poppy's mental health was no longer an issue. Whatever crime had been committed had absolutely nothing to do with her and there was really nothing else holding her here.

Still, maybe she'd stick around another couple days just until Benjamin thought it was safe for Poppy to return to his own house. Her decision to stay had nothing to do with the fact that Benjamin's chocolate-colored eyes made her yearn for things she knew better than to wish for, nothing to do with the fact that his kiss had stirred her on levels she'd never felt before.

It was just after the three of them had eaten lunch when Edie stepped out the front door and sat in one of the two wicker chairs on the porch. The afternoon sun was unusually warm and the air held the scents of fresh hay, rich earth and fall leaves.

In the distance she could see a herd of cattle grazing and several horses frolicking in circles. Peaceful. The scene, the entire place, felt peaceful and enduring.

It would be a wonderful place to raise a family and it wasn't a stretch to think that Benjamin would make a terrific father.

He'd shown incredible patience with Poppy and his affection of his dog spoke of a man who could love easily. Love and patience, the most important things that children needed to grow up healthy.

She reached to hold the charm that dangled in the hollow of her throat. It was cold, like the shell that surrounded her heart.

He was a man who deserved children and that was just another reason for her to steer clear of him. There would be no children in her future.

As she gazed out she saw a plume of dust rising in the air, indicating a vehicle was approaching. She steadfastly ignored the quickened beat of her heart as Benjamin's truck came into view.

She remained seated as he parked and got out of the pickup, his weariness evident in the stress lines down his face and the slight slump of his shoulders. Still, he offered her a warm smile as he stepped onto the porch.

"Long night," she said as he eased down in the chair next to hers.

"You have no idea." He pulled a hand through his hair, messing it up and yet only managing to look carelessly sexy.

"Can you tell me what you found?" She found it difficult to look at him as the sleepy cast to his eyes only made him look sexier and brought to her mind the memory of the kiss they'd shared.

"You won't believe it. I still don't believe it myself." He drew in a deep breath and released it with a sigh. "We found an arm, a foot and a hand each buried in the clearing and all of them glowing like they could power a car for ten years."

Edie sucked in her breath in shock. "Do they belong to somebody who was murdered?"

"We think the arm belongs to Jim Taylor. He died of cancer and had a proper burial a little over a week ago. We don't know who the other hand belongs to, although it's definitely female. And we don't know about the foot."

She stared at him in stunned surprise. "And you don't know why they were glowing like that?"

He shook his head. "My brother Jacob arranged for a contact at the FBI lab in Topeka and Sam McCain, one of the other deputies, is transporting them there as we speak."

"What do you think it all means?" She fought the impulse to reach out and stroke her hand across his furrowed brow. He looked as if the weight of the world suddenly rested on his shoulders.

"It's too early to be able to tell what any of it means," he replied. "But we're wondering if maybe somebody is conducting some sort of experiments on Black Rock's dead."

Edie fought the chill that attempted to waltz up her back. "Any suspects?"

He barked a humorless laugh. "At the moment, only everyone in town." He sighed again, a weary sound that blew through her.

"Why do you do this?" she asked curiously.

He turned and looked at her. "Do what?"

"Why are you a deputy? It's obvious that your heart is here at the ranch. Even Poppy said he doesn't understand why you aren't ranching full-time."

He gazed out in the distance and shrugged. "Working law enforcement is what we Grayson men do. Sure, I love the ranch, but in this town, people know me as a man with a badge. That's who I am." He said the words almost belligerently, as if he were trying to convince himself of something rather than her. "So, how has your day been?"

"Okay, although there seems to be a territorial

war going on over the kitchen. I thought Poppy and Margaret might come to blows over who was going to fix lunch."

"Who won?" He leaned back in the chair and some of the tension in his shoulders appeared to ease.

"Definitely Margaret. In fact she threatened to blacken his other eye if he touched one of her pots or pans."

He smiled then, a tired smile that erased the worried lines that had tracked across his forehead. "I'm not surprised. She's a feisty one."

"There seems to be some strange energy between her and Poppy. It's like they're kids and he pulls her hair and she kicks him in the shin but beneath all the aggression is some kind of crazy attraction."

"They've both been alone for a long time. I think it would be great if they hooked up."

"I can't believe we're talking about my grandfather *hooking up*," she said drily.

He laughed but quickly his laughter died and he gazed at her with smoldering eyes. "It would be nice if somebody around here was hooking up."

For a moment gazing into his eyes she felt as if she couldn't breathe. It took conscious willpower to force herself to look away from him but it was impossible for her to reply.

"I need to get some sleep," he said. "I have a feeling as this case unfolds it's going to take all the energy we have to give." He stood and once again looked weary beyond words.

"Aren't you afraid of nightmares?" she asked as she also got up from her chair.

He took a step closer to her, so close their bodies almost touched. Once again her breath caught in her chest as he reached up and touched a strand of her hair. "There's only one thing that would definitely keep nightmares at bay, and that's if you were in bed with me as my snuggle buddy."

He dropped his hand and stepped back from her. "But since you've indicated that's not happening, then the best I can do is hope that my dreams are pleasant." He didn't wait for a reply but instead turned and went into the house.

She stared after him and finally released a shuddering sigh. For just a moment as she'd gazed into those magnetic eyes of his, as she'd felt the heat of his body radiating out to warm hers, she'd wanted to be his snuggle buddy. And that scared her almost as much as eerie, glowing body parts buried in the woods.

"Can you tell me where you were Wednesday night around one in the morning?" Benjamin asked Abe Appleton, the local retired chemist. Abe's current claim to fame in the town came from the programs he presented to elementary-school classes about chemistry and physics.

"On any given night at one in the morning I assure you I can be found in my bed," Abe said. "Is this about that mess on Moreland's property? Why on earth would you think I had anything to do with that?"

"We're talking to anyone in town who has a background in chemistry," Benjamin replied. The two men stood on Abe's porch. It was just after eight in the morning.

When Benjamin had arrived in the office that morning, Tom had handed him a list of people he wanted Benjamin to interview. Abe had been the first name on the list.

Deputies were still working the clearing, digging to see if there were any other surprises buried there. It would be days before they heard back from the FBI lab on what exactly had caused the glow to the body parts, but the investigation was ongoing.

The small-town rumor mill was working overtime with the gossip ranging from a serial killer in their midst to a mad scientist conducting unholy experiments on murder victims.

"You want to come in, check my alibi with Violet? She sleeps light and would know if I wasn't in bed on the night in question," Abe said. "Benjamin, I make volcanoes out of baking soda for the kids. I suck a hard-boiled egg into a bottle. I have no idea what happened in the woods."

"You know anyone else who might have a background in chemistry?" Benjamin asked.

Abe frowned thoughtfully. "Not off the top of my head. 'Course I don't know exactly what you found. When Violet and I were at the café early this morning, we heard everything from a leg that got up and danced on its own to a hand that grabbed Tom around the throat."

Benjamin grinned. "Sounds fascinating, but it's hardly close to the truth." His grin faded as he considered the truth. "Still, it looks like somebody was doing some sort of experimenting, somebody who might have a background in either medicine or chemistry."

"Can't think of anyone, but if I do I know where to contact you," Abe replied.

"Thanks, Abe. I may be back with more questions."

Abe smiled. "In that case you know where to contact me."

Minutes later as Benjamin backed out of Abe's driveway, he thought of all the arms this investigation entailed. While he was interviewing potential suspects, Caleb was following up with Josh Willoughby at the cemetery. There was no question that the arm they'd unearthed belonged to old Jim Taylor and that meant, at the very least, that there was some grave-robbing going on.

Tom had another deputy assigned to checking the sales of hazmat suits. The suits were not cheap and hopefully they'd get a lead through that avenue.

A different deputy was assigned to interview doctors and nurses at the hospital. Since they didn't know what they were dealing with there was no way of knowing if they were spinning their wheels or not.

As he headed toward the taxidermy store in town, his thoughts turned to Edie, who was never really out of his mind. He was thirty years old and more than ready to be in love, ready to start a family. He wanted to fill the house with children who he could teach to love the ranch as much as he did.

Edie had asked him why he wasn't ranching full-time and Benjamin hadn't been completely honest with her. The truth was he was afraid of what was beneath his badge, afraid that there might be nothing.

Being a deputy gave him a sense of purpose and more than a little respect in the town. Without that what would he be? What would he have?

He dismissed the crazy thoughts from his head as he parked in front of the taxidermy shop. When they had been making the list of people to interview, Abe's name had come to mind first because of his background in chemistry, and after some careful thought Big Jeff Hudson and his son, Little Jeff, were added to the list. None of the deputies had any idea what kind of chemicals were used in the taxidermy business, but Benjamin intended to find out now.

A tinkling bell above the door announced his arrival as he stepped into the shop. This was his least favorite place in town. Dead animals stared at him from all directions. He found the whole thing rather creepy.

"Benjamin!" Big Jeff greeted him from behind the counter in the back of the store. "What a surprise. I rarely see you in here."

Benjamin made his way around a standing deer to approach the thin, older man. "How's business?"

"Not great, but we'll be swamped soon with deer

season opening. What brings you into my little shop of horrors?"

"I need to ask you some questions. I suppose you've heard about the crime scene on Moreland's property."

"Is anyone talking about anything else?"

"It does seem to be the topic of the day," Benjamin agreed. "Is Little Jeff around?"

"He's in the back unloading some supplies, but he doesn't like to be called Little Jeff anymore. He goes by Jeffrey Allen now. You want me to get him?"

Benjamin nodded and immediately thought about the key fob he'd found by the bush at the cemetery the morning after Walt's beating. *A* for Abe? For Allen? The idea of either man beating the hell out of Walt seemed a stretch, but Benjamin wasn't about to close off his mind to any possibility.

Big Jeff disappeared into the back room and returned a moment later followed by his son. It had been years since the nickname of Little Jeff had been appropriate for the hulking thirty-four-year-old who had been primed to take over the family business when Big Jeff retired.

"Hey, Benjamin," Jeffrey Allen greeted him with a friendly smile. "Dad said you wanted to talk to me. What's up?"

"I wanted to ask the two of you about the chemicals you use in processing animals. Any of them considered toxic?"

"By no stretch of the imagination," Big Jeff replied easily.

"Any of them contain some sort of fluorescent properties?"

Jeffrey Allen laughed. "Not hardly. I don't know one of the local hunters or fishermen who want their prize catch to glow in the dark."

By the time Benjamin left the shop he knew more about taxidermy than he'd ever wanted to know. The rest of the day was more of the same, asking questions of people and getting nothing substantial to help with the case.

It was going to be difficult to pin down alibis of anyone they might suspect for the night that Walt and Edie had been confronted in the woods. At that time of night most people would say they were in bed asleep and that was difficult to disprove.

After talking to the people on his list, he returned to the office, where he was updated by his brother Tom. There had been nothing else found in the clearing and Devon Moreland had claimed complete ignorance on what had been happening there.

The bullet that had shattered Edie's rear window had come from a .38 caliber handgun, definitely common to this area. Tom had assigned one of the other deputies to check gun and ATV owners in the area but it would be several days before he'd have a definitive list.

He'd made arrangements for Edie's back car window to be replaced that morning.

It was just after seven when he finally made his way to the ranch. Weariness pulled at his muscles and hunger pangs filled his belly. Breakfast had been a muffin and a cup of coffee and he'd skipped lunch. He was sure that Margaret would have a plate waiting for him when he got home.

As he approached the house he saw Edie sitting on the porch, the last of the day's sunshine sparking in her hair. Pleasure swelled up inside him, banishing any thought of food or rest.

He could get used to coming home to her. There was no question that she touched him on all kinds of levels. As he parked his truck and got out, she rose from the chair and smiled.

That smile of hers eased some of his weariness and replaced it with a simmering desire to learn more about her, to taste her mouth once again, to somehow get beneath the defenses she'd wrapped around herself.

"Long day," she said. It was a comment, not a question.

"I have a feeling they're all going to be long for a while."

"Anything new?"

He shook his head. "Nothing specific. Let's get inside. It's too cool to sit out here once the sun goes down."

The second he opened the door Tiny greeted him with a happy dance that had both him and Edie laughing. "He's become my buddy when you're gone," she said as Benjamin bent down and picked up Tiny.

"Do you like dogs?"

"I love Tiny," she replied. "Where did you get him?"

"Found him in a box on the side of the road. Somebody had dumped him. He was half-dead and I wasn't sure he was going to make it but all he needed was a little tender loving care."

Edie stepped closer to him and scratched Tiny behind one of his ears. "Poor little thing. I wonder if he has nightmares about the bad things that happened to him before you found him."

"I like to think that with enough time and love, bad memories no longer hold the power to give you nightmares," he replied. It didn't escape his notice that this was the second time she'd mentioned nightmares, making him wonder what haunted her sleep at night.

They walked from the living room into the kitchen, where Margaret and Walt were seated at the table with cups of coffee. Margaret jumped up at the sight of him. "The rest of us already ate, but I've got a bowl of beef stew all ready for you, along with some corn bread that will stick to your ribs."

"Thanks, Margaret." Benjamin set Tiny down on the floor and then went to the sink to wash up to eat. "Walt, that eye is looking better," he said once he was seated at the table. "How are the ribs?"

"Still sore, but not as bad as they were. Have you caught the creep who beat me up yet?"

Benjamin was aware of Edie sliding into the chair next to him, the spicy scent of her filling him with a hunger for something other than beef stew. "Not yet, but we're working on it," he said to Walt.

For the next few minutes, as he ate, he told them what he could about the investigation. He finished eating and

Margaret took his plates away and then announced that she and Walt were going to her cottage to play some rummy.

"I think we'll know more about everything when we get some results back from the FBI lab," he said to Edie once the older people had left the house.

"But that could take a while, right?"

"Unfortunately," he agreed with a nod of his head. "In the meantime we'll keep interviewing people and hope that somebody knows something about what's been going on."

Edie leaned back in her chair. She looked as pretty as he'd ever seen her in a deep pink sweater that enhanced her coloring. "I think it's time I go home."

"Do you really think that's a good idea?"

"Whoever chased us the other night must realize by now that we couldn't identify them. Plus I know that Poppy isn't crazy and he's insisting I go home."

He wanted to protest. He wanted to ask her if she'd stay for him. But they'd shared only a single kiss and he really had no right to ask her to stay.

"So what are your plans?"

"I'll stop over at Poppy's place in the morning and get my things and then head on back to Topeka." She frowned. "I hate to leave him like this and I was wondering if it would be okay with you if Poppy remains here a couple of days. He is healing nicely, but I think the attack shook him up more than he's saying. I tried to tell him I wanted to stay at least until he gets back on his feet, but he went ballistic."

"He's welcome to stay until he feels like he's ready to go home," Benjamin said.

She nodded. "I appreciate it."

"And if I need to talk to you? About the investigation?"

"I'll give you my cell phone number and when I get settled in a new place, I'll let you know my address."

"I'll be sorry to see you go." The words escaped him before he realized he intended to speak them.

Her gaze didn't quite meet his. "You're a nice man, Benjamin, and you deserve a nice woman in your life." She got up from the table. "Believe me, I'm the last person on earth you need in your life in any way. I'm not a nice woman and it's time for me to get back to my life."

Before he could respond she turned and left the kitchen.

Chapter 7

It was after eleven when Edie finally left Benjamin's ranch the next morning. Margaret had insisted she have a big breakfast and it had been difficult to say goodbye to both her and Poppy.

She might have stuck around if she thought that Poppy really needed her, but she sensed a bit of romance taking place between him and Margaret, a romance that could fill any loneliness Poppy might have entertained.

Benjamin had already been gone when she'd gotten out of bed and she'd remained in her room the night before after she'd left him in the kitchen.

She'd been afraid to spend any more time around him, afraid that somehow he'd talk her into staying, afraid that he might kiss her again and made her want him even more deeply than she already did. It was definitely time to get out of Dodge, but her heart was heavy as the ranch disappeared in her rearview mirror.

She could have been happy there, she could be happy with Benjamin, if she deserved happiness. But deep in her soul she knew the truth.

Still, she was grateful she hadn't had to face him one last time that morning. It was easier this way, with no long, drawn-out goodbyes.

By the time she entered the outskirts of town she was thinking of the problems that awaited her in Topeka. Thank God she had a little bit of savings put away, just enough to get her into another small apartment.

She wasn't too worried about a job. She'd flip hamburgers if necessary to get by until she found something more permanent. It would have been nice if she'd gone to college, but there had never been enough money at home, and the minute she'd graduated from high school she'd started working to help out her mother.

When she reached Poppy's place she parked in the driveway and got out of the car, surprised when a neighbor hurried out of his house and toward her.

"Hi," he said with a smile of friendliness. "I'm Bart Crosswell, Walt's neighbor. I was just wondering how he's doing. Me and my wife heard about him getting beaten up but we haven't seen him since then."

Bart was about sixty with a broad face that looked as if it had never held a frown. "He's staying with some friends for the next couple days," she replied, "but he's doing just fine."

"Glad to hear that. And I noticed you cleaned up the yard real nice. We didn't want to complain or say anything, but it was obvious that it had kind of gotten away from him over the past few months."

"I'll try to make sure that somebody is keeping on top of it from now on," Edie said, grateful that the neighbor appeared to be a nice guy.

"I don't mind mowing it whenever I mow my own. I just didn't want to step on Walt's toes," Bart said.

"That's very kind of you. When he gets back home maybe the two of you can work out an agreeable arrangement," she replied.

"Will do." He lifted a hand in a friendly goodbye and then began to walk back to his house.

Poppy would be fine, Edie thought as she let herself into the house. He had friends and neighbors that obviously cared about him. He didn't need her. Nobody needed her and she didn't need anyone, she reminded herself as she climbed the stairs.

She pulled her overnight bag from the closet and set it on the bed. It wouldn't take long for her to gather her things and leave town.

Leave Benjamin. She couldn't help the little pang in her heart as she thought about him. In another place, in another time, she might have allowed herself to care about him. But, she couldn't think about that now.

She went into the bathroom across the hall and gathered the toiletries she hadn't taken to Benjamin's and then returned to the bedroom and placed them in her overnight bag.

Once she had all her clothes folded and packed away, she sat on the edge of the bed and allowed herself to think about Benjamin once again.

He'd asked her if she'd considered relocating to Black Rock now that there was really nothing holding her to Topeka. In the brief time she'd been here as an adult, she recognized that Black Rock was a pleasant town filled with friendly people.

It was easy to imagine living in Black Rock. She could get an apartment close enough to the downtown area that she could walk to the stores on nice days. She could enjoy regular visits with Poppy and build a pleasant life here.

There was only one fly in the ointment: a hot sexy deputy with soft brown eyes and hot kisses that made her want to forget her vow of celibacy, forget that she'd given up on finding any real happiness.

No, she wouldn't even consider relocating here. Benjamin Grayson was too much temptation and believing she could ever have a loving relationship with anyone was nothing but utter foolishness.

She rose from the bed and froze as she heard it—the soft, but unmistakable creak of the third step. Her blood chilled as she realized somebody else was in the house, somebody who hadn't announced their presence but was quietly creeping up the staircase.

Her breathing went shallow as she grabbed her purse and shot a wild gaze around the room, seeking something that might be used as a weapon.

There was nothing. And as she heard the distinct

creak of the seventh step panic clawed at her. There was no question in her mind that whoever it was had no good intentions, otherwise they would have said something to announce their presence.

Clutching her purse, she silently moved across the room and into the closet. She closed the closet door and sat on the floor with her back against it and her legs braced on the other side.

For a long moment she heard nothing but the frantic bang of her own heartbeat. God, she'd been careless. She hadn't locked the front door behind her when she'd come inside. She hadn't thought there was any danger.

If it were Bart surely he would say something. Agonizing moments ticked by and she heard nothing. Her heart rate began to slow a bit. Had she only imagined those creaks? Had it just been the house settling?

At that moment a fist crashed into the closet door. "Come out of there, you bitch," a deep voice snarled.

Edie swallowed a scream and pressed her back more firmly against the door. Help. She needed help. Oh, God, her cell phone.

She wildly fumbled in the bottom of her purse for her cell phone. A deep sob escaped her as she scrabbled to find the instrument that would bring help.

He grabbed the door handle and turned it, then threw himself against the door with a force that shook the door frame. "You and that old man ruined everything! I'm going to make you pay if it's the last thing I do."

Deep and guttural. She didn't recognize the voice.

As he slammed into the door once again she managed to get hold of her cell phone.

"I'm calling the sheriff," she cried out as she punched 9-1-1.

When the operator answered she gave them Poppy's address and then screamed as the door shuddered once again.

"You won't get away from me no matter where you go." The voice shimmered with rage. "I'll find you wherever you are and make you pay for screwing up my life." There was a snap of wood as the frame broke and then silence.

The only noise was her gasping breaths and uncontrollable sobs. Was he gone? Or was it a trick? Was he waiting for her to venture out of the closet so he could hurt her? She shoved the back of her fist against her mouth as tears blurred her vision.

Who had it been? And what had she done to warrant such intense hatred? Would she be safe going back to Topeka or would he find her there to merit out some form of twisted revenge?

Benjamin was grabbing a quick cup of coffee in the café when he heard the call for a responder to Walt's address. He tore out of the building and jumped into his car, his heart hammering so fast he could scarcely catch his breath.

There could only be one person who would have made that call. Edie. He knew she'd be stopping by

Walt's on her way out of town, although he hadn't known specifically what time she might be leaving.

If anything happened to her, he'd never forgive himself. He should have talked her out of leaving town, insisted that she stick around until they had a handle on the whole situation.

It took only minutes for him to arrive at Walt's. He went through the open front door with his gun drawn, anticipating trouble.

He heard nothing. The silence of the house thundered in his head as he slowly made his way from room to room. He didn't want to call out. If somebody was inside, he didn't want to announce his presence or exacerbate whatever the situation might be. He damn sure didn't want to force somebody to hurt Edie.

When he'd cleared the lower level of the house he crept up the stairs, wincing as two of them creaked beneath his weight. When he reached the first bedroom, his heatbeat crashed so hard in his ears he feared he wouldn't hear anything else.

He cleared the bedrooms and bathroom until there was only one left at the end of the hallway. His heart jumped into his throat as he saw Edie's overnight bag on the bed. He finally called out, "It's Deputy Grayson. Is anyone here?"

She exploded out of the closet and into his embrace. Trembling arms wrapped around his neck and she buried her face in his chest and began to weep.

He held her tight with one arm and his gun with the other. "What happened?"

"He was here. He said I ruined everything and he was going to make me pay." The words escaped her on a trail of tears as she squeezed her arms around his neck.

"Who, honey? Who was it?"

"I don't know. I didn't see him."

He felt her physically pull herself together. A single deep breath and she moved out of his embrace. But her face was achingly pale and her eyes were wide and red-rimmed from her tears.

"I had just finished packing when I heard somebody on the stairs." Her voice trembled. "I got scared. Thank God I grabbed my purse and hid in the closet." Tears welled up in her eyes once again. "I sat on the floor and braced myself as he started to slam into the door. I thought he was going to get in before anyone got here to help."

"Let's get you out of here," he said. As she grabbed her purse from the closet, he picked up her overnight bag and wondered who in the hell had come after her.

"We're going to the sheriff's office to file a report and then I'm taking you back to the ranch," he said once they were in his car. "You aren't heading out of town by yourself until I'm certain that you're no longer in danger."

"If you're expecting an argument, you aren't going to get one," she replied.

"You didn't recognize his voice?"

She shook her head. "It was just a deep growl." She wrapped her arms around herself as if to fight off a shiver. "He sounded so angry, like he would easily enjoy strangling me to death with his bare hands."

Benjamin tightened his hands on the steering wheel as a rage began inside him. The idea of anyone putting their hands on Edie made a rich anger burn in his gut.

When they arrived at the sheriff's office, Tom sat down with them and Edie told him what had occurred. Tom immediately dispatched two deputies to Walt's house to fingerprint the closet and talk to Bart. They hoped Bart might have seen whoever entered the house.

Confident that the investigation side of things was under control, within an hour Benjamin and Edie were back in his car and headed to the ranch.

"I know you were eager to return to Topeka and get things settled there," he said.

"Funny how somebody trying to kill you can change your mind." She offered him a weak smile.

A healthy dose of respect for her filled him.

"I have this terrible fear that if I go back to Topeka now this creep will somehow find me there and I won't have my own personal deputy to ride to my rescue," she added.

Benjamin tried to find a responding smile, but there was absolutely nothing humorous about the situation. "I shouldn't have let you go," he said. "I shouldn't have let you go to Walt's to get your things alone. I should have been with you or I should have talked you out of leaving altogether."

She reached out and placed her hand on his arm.

"How could you know that I might be in danger? Who could know that he'd be after revenge for me somehow screwing things up for him. I just wish I knew what it is he thinks I messed up." She removed her hand from his arm.

"If we knew that, we'd probably have all the answers." Benjamin wheeled through the entrance that led to the ranch. He didn't want to tell her that the thing that worried him now was that whoever had come after her would eventually know she and Walt were staying here.

If it came down to him doing his job or keeping her safe, the job could go to hell. He'd already lost one woman in his life. Brittany. He had no hope of ever seeing his sister again.

Edie had made it clear to him that she didn't want him in her life on any kind of a romantic basis, but his heart was already taken by her and the idea of anything happening to her nearly shattered him.

"You'll be safe at the ranch, both you and Walt. I'll make sure of it," he said firmly.

"I don't doubt that at all," she replied.

As Benjamin parked in front of the ranch his mind whirled with all the ways he could assure their safety. Tom certainly didn't have men to spare given the magnitude of the current investigation.

Maybe it was time to have a talk with Jacob, see if he could enlist his brother's help in keeping an eye on the ranch.

When they got into the house Benjamin sat down with

Walt, Margaret and Edie and told them how important it was that the house remained locked at all times, that they keep an eye out for trouble and that obviously the threat to Edie and Walt wasn't over.

He didn't anticipate any trouble immediately, so after making sure all the doors were locked up tight, Benjamin left to go talk to his brother.

Jacob had holed himself up in a small cabin on the property almost three months earlier. He'd quit his job in Kansas City with the FBI and had come home with deep haunting shadows in his eyes and had refused to discuss with anyone what had happened to him.

The only thing he'd told his brothers when he'd arrived in Black Rock was that he didn't want anyone to know he was back. He lived like a hermit and Benjamin and Margaret provided the supplies he needed.

It took only minutes for Benjamin to pull up in front of the cabin that was nearly hidden in a thick grove of trees. At one time this had been a caretaker's cabin, but during Benjamin's childhood it had been used as a guest cottage and an occasional romantic getaway for his parents.

He found his brother where he always found him, in the small living room in a recliner with a beer in his hand and the television playing.

Jacob's cheeks and chin were covered with whisker stubble and his dark hair was longer than Benjamin had ever seen it. He looked like a man without pride, a man who had lost the ability to care about anything.

"You look like hell," Benjamin said as he came through the front door.

"And a good afternoon to you, too, little brother." Jacob gestured him into the chair opposite him and turned down the volume on the television. "What's going on?"

"I need your help." Benjamin eased down into the chair.

Jacob raised one of his dark eyebrows. "I hope it doesn't require me leaving this chair or my beer."

A flash of irritation swept through Benjamin. He'd always looked up to Jacob but the shell of a man who had returned to the ranch was nothing like the man who had left.

"Actually, it does require you getting away from the beer and out of your chair," Benjamin said.

"Then the odds of me being able to help you out are pretty slim."

"For God's sake, Jacob. Pull yourself together," Benjamin exclaimed with a burst of uncharacteristic anger. "I need you to help me keep a woman safe."

Jacob took a sip of his beer and eyed Benjamin with interest. "Something in your voice tells me this is a special woman."

Benjamin felt a faint heat crawl into his cheeks. "She's in trouble through no fault of her own. Somebody attacked her today and I don't think the perp is finished yet. I've got her at the house but I'd like an extra pair of eyes watching things there."

"Does this have to do with the Moreland mess?"

Benjamin nodded. "I've got both Walt Tolliver and his granddaughter at the house." He leaned back in the chair and released a sigh. "I'd assumed since they couldn't identify the culprits that they were safe from harm. But I was wrong." He told his brother what had taken place at Walt's house.

"So he didn't go after her to somehow protect himself. He went after her for revenge." Jacob shook his head. "That's a nasty motive for an attack. I'd say whoever you're looking for has a history of a short fuse, maybe some sort of persecution complex. You know the type, the whole world is against him and whatever troubles he has is always somebody else's fault."

"Not much of a profile to go on," Benjamin said.

Jacob shrugged. "Not much information yet to go on. Tom called me last night to give me the latest on what's been happening with the case."

"Right now my main concern is keeping Walt and Edie safe. I'm hoping Tom can spare me so I can hang out at the house, but I'd feel better knowing you had my back."

Jacob set his beer down and his eyes were as black as night. "I got your back," he said simply. "Just let me know when you need me around and I'll be there."

"Are you ever going to tell me what brought you home?" Benjamin asked softly. Jacob broke eye contact and for a long moment said nothing. Benjamin leaned forward in his chair. "Whatever it is, Jacob, we can help you."

His brother looked at him with a wry smile. "Nobody can help me."

"Just tell me this. Are you hiding from somebody or are you hiding from yourself?"

Jacob's eyes widened and then narrowed into slits. "Maybe a little bit of both." He picked up his bottle of beer once again. "Just give me a call if you need me to keep an eye on the house." He picked up the remote control and turned up the volume on the television in an obvious dismissal.

As Benjamin headed back to the ranch house he couldn't help but worry about his brother. He felt as if they'd already lost Brittany and if something wasn't done, somehow they were going to lose Jacob.

It wasn't right for a man to wall himself off from everyone. It wasn't right for a man to be alone with just his beer and his thoughts. Jacob needed something, but until he asked for it nobody could give it to him.

As he once again parked in front of the house and got out of the truck, his thoughts turned to the woman inside. For some reason he felt as if she and Jacob shared that common trait. He thought that Edie needed something from somebody but was afraid or refused to ask.

He only wished it was him that she needed, that she wanted. But he had resigned himself to the fact that the only thing he could do for her was to keep her safe. And when the danger passed, he would send her off to live her life without him.

Chapter 8

Edgy.

That was the only word to describe what Edie felt as she sat in the kitchen. It had been two days since the attack on her, two days of confinement with Benjamin. He hadn't left the house or her side for the past forty-eight hours.

She'd been in bed, but had gotten up a few minutes ago and decided to make herself a cup of hot tea.

She sat at the table with the hot brew in front of her with only the oven light on. This was the first time she felt as if she could breathe, without his overwhelming presence by her side.

Familiarity was supposed to breed contempt, but in this case that old adage was wrong. The sexual tension between them had grown to mammoth proportions. She felt his hot, simmering gaze on her like a hand on her thigh, a palm on her breast, and with each moment that passed she wanted it, wanted him.

And in the past two days Margaret and Poppy had become best buddies, sharing the kitchen like two top chefs, playing card games and giggling like teenagers.

She felt a desperate need to get out of town, but each time she thought about leaving all she could think about was that man hunting her down and making her pay.

There was no question that being here in this house with Benjamin made her feel safe. He'd even insisted Margaret move into the bedroom across the hall from Walt's for the time being rather than stay in her little cottage behind the house. He didn't want anyone to somehow use her to get to Poppy and Edie.

She leaned forward in the chair and took a sip of her tea that warmed her all the way down to her toes. No matter how she tried to keep thoughts of Benjamin at bay, he continued to intrude into her brain.

As if summoned by her thoughts alone, he appeared in the doorway of the kitchen, Tiny at his feet. "I thought you were asleep," she said.

He moved from the doorway to the table and sat next to her. Tiny curled up on the rug between them. "I was on the phone with Tom getting updates."

"So what's new?"

"Not enough to solve the case," he said with frustration. "We know now that the arm definitely belonged to Jim Taylor, the old man I told you about who died of cancer. The other two body parts still haven't been identified. We haven't heard anything from the FBI lab on what chemicals might have been involved."

"Then there's really no news," she said and lifted her cup for another sip of tea.

He forced a smile. "Nothing concrete but they're all gathering information that hopefully will eventually crack the case."

"You should be back in the office instead of hanging around here with me," she said.

"Right now you and Walt are our best clues to what might be happening. If somebody comes after you here, I'll be ready for them. I'm doing my job by making sure you and Walt are safe."

"How come you don't have any workers around here?" she asked curiously. She'd noticed that she never saw anyone in the yard or in the pastures or corral.

"I'm a small operation. I've been able to handle things myself for the past couple of years."

"Tell me about your sister." She'd been curious about the woman who had gone missing, a woman he barely mentioned. "What's she like?"

For just a brief moment a smile curved his lips and his eyes warmed. "Beautiful, impulsive and headstrong. We all spoiled her terribly. But she's also bright and tough and has a great sense of humor."

His smile fell and his eyes darkened. He placed a hand on the table, his long fingers splayed on the top and stared down. "She was working as a deputy like the rest of us. Initially when she missed work none of us panicked. She'd occasionally oversleep or get screwed up with her schedule and forget to come in until we called her. It wasn't until a full day went by with no word from her that we all started to get a little concerned."

He leaned forward and his fingers curled into a tight fist. "By the time two days had gone by with no word from her, we knew she was in trouble. There had been no activity in her bank account, her cell phone wasn't picking up and that's when true panic set in."

She was sorry she'd asked, saw the pain that radiated from his features and compressed his lips tightly together. Her heart ached with his pain but before she could find words to comfort him, he continued speaking.

"I can't explain to you what it felt like when the realization struck that she had met with foul play. Suddenly every minute that passed was sheer torture. It was impossible to eat, impossible to sleep. I tried making deals with fate. You know, if she'd just show up safe and sound then I could be struck dead. If she would just be returned to us then fate could take this ranch from me and I'd happily live in a hovel for the rest of my life." He released a short, strained laugh. "God, I've never told anyone this stuff."

She reached across the table and covered his fisted hand with her own. "I'm sorry, Benjamin. I can't imagine what it must be like to not know what happened to somebody you love."

He uncurled his hand and instead entwined his fingers with hers. "Eventually the gut-ripping desperation passes and you find that you have to eat, you have to sleep, that life goes on no matter what." He gazed at her with sad eyes. "My brothers all hold on to the hope that she'll eventually be found alive, but not me. The day we found her car hidden in an old abandoned barn, my gut told me she's dead."

For a moment Edie didn't know what to say to comfort him, but her need to take the pain from his eyes was visceral. She understood his grief, awakened with her own each morning and went to bed with it each night. "I'm sorry, Benjamin. I'm so sorry that you're going through this."

He tightened his grip on her hand. "Thanks. It actually helped to talk about it. Now, why don't you tell me what puts the sadness in your eyes?"

She forced a laugh and gently pulled her hand from his. "Life," she said. "My life really started to crumble when my mother died." Edie once again wrapped her hands around her teacup. "We were very best friends. My father walked out on us when I was just a baby and it was always just her and me."

"She never thought about remarrying?" he asked.

"Not that I know of. I don't think she ever dated. She had a circle of girlfriends and when she wasn't with them, she seemed content alone. I met Greg in a bar two weeks after Mom's death."

She paused to take a sip of the tea that was now lukewarm. There was something intensely intimate about sitting at the table with everyone else in bed. In the semidarkness of the kitchen it seemed easier to let her guard down, to open herself up to him.

"I was grieving and vulnerable and ripe for the

picking. He moved in and I became one of those too-stupid-to-live women I abhor. I made every mistake a woman can make. I believed whatever he told me about his money being tied up in some high dollar business. He fed me what I needed to hear but it was nothing but lies." She shrugged and offered him a crooked smile. "It felt tragic at the time he left me, but now I realize he did me a big favor by getting out of my life. I'm like my mother. I'm good alone."

Benjamin's gaze lingered for a long moment on her face. "I wish I'd met you first," he finally said softly. "I wish I'd been the man in your life before Greg ever entered it."

There it was, that deep yearning to fall into his gaze, to feel his strong arms wrapped around her, his heartbeat against her own. It was a palpable want, melting something inside her she didn't want melted.

"It wouldn't have made a difference," she said, surprised that her voice didn't sound strong and sure, but rather breathy and faint.

He leaned back in his chair and released a sigh. "Tell me what gives you nightmares."

She looked at him in surprise and gave an uneasy laugh. "What makes you think I have nightmares?"

"I don't know, I've just had the impression that you do."

"Staying up too late and drinking tea gives me nightmares about tea bags," she said as she got up from the table. She carried her cup to the sink, aware of his gaze remaining on her.

She rinsed the cup and placed it in the dishwasher and then turned to face him once again. "Don't, Benjamin. Don't pry to find out any secrets I might have, the kind of woman I am. Trust me when I tell you that you wouldn't like what you uncovered."

"I find that hard to believe," he replied as she walked toward the kitchen door.

"Good night, Benjamin," she said and then left the kitchen. As she went through the living room toward the hallway she fought against the sudden sear of hot tears at her eyes.

The charm around her neck seemed to burn her skin, a painful reminder of loss and grief. It had been her fault. She should have never gotten pregnant. She obviously wasn't meant to be a mother.

Even though the doctor had told her that sometimes these things happened for no discernible reason, when the baby died Edie had known the truth, that somehow she was responsible, that it had been her fault that her baby had been born dead.

Benjamin deserved better. He deserved more than she'd ever be able to give him. She had no intention of having children. She had no intention of ever loving again.

She would admit it, she was a coward. She didn't want to risk the chance of loss once again. Even with a man like Benjamin. Especially with a man like Benjamin.

As much as it pained her, she had to keep him out of her heart.

* * *

It had been another long day. After the discussion with Edie the night before, Benjamin had gone to bed with a heavy heart.

He felt that over the past several days he'd gotten to know her as well as he'd ever known any woman. She was kind and warm and giving. She had a wonderful sense of humor and was bright and so achingly beautiful. And yet, he sensed a darkness in her that he couldn't pierce.

She'd been distant with him all day, as if punishing him for getting too close the night before. Tension had sparked in the air between them until he'd felt he might explode.

The tension had eased when after dinner the four of them had sat at the table and played poker. The laughter the games created was a welcome relief.

There was no doubt that there were sparks between Walt and Margaret. They had begun to act like a couple who had been married for fifty years, finishing each other's sentences and exchanging warm gazes. He had a feeling when this was all over and done he might just lose his housekeeper, but he couldn't feel bad about it. He was only glad that Walt and Margaret had found each other to share companionship in the golden years of their lives.

He now sat in his recliner, Tiny on his lap. Edie had gone into Walt's bedroom to check the wrap around his ribs and Margaret had gone to bed.

A man needed companionship. Men weren't wired to

be alone and he believed Edie wasn't wired to be alone, either. There was no question in his mind that she was attracted to him, that she had feelings for him. He knew it in her gaze, felt it in her touch, sensed it radiating from her as they warily circled one another.

But he didn't know how to get beneath her defenses. He didn't have the tools to know how to get to her heart. Tiny whined, as if sensing Benjamin's growing despondency.

"Shhh." He scrubbed the dog beneath his ear, which instantly halted the whine. Too bad a scratch behind Benjamin's ear wouldn't solve the depression he felt settling around his shoulders like an old, heavy shawl.

Maybe the problem was a lack of sleep, he told himself. He felt as if he needed to be on duty twenty-four hours a day and he'd only been catching catnaps throughout the long nights.

Most of the hours of the night he wandered from window to window, looking outside, wondering if danger lurked anywhere near.

For the moment the investigation was proceeding without him, although he'd kept in close contact with both Tom and Caleb. It was impossible to trace ATVs through motor vehicle records because they were for off-road use. But Sam McCain had come up with a list of people they all knew had the vehicles in town.

Jim Ramsey, another deputy, was checking gun records and collecting the names of everyone who owned a .38 caliber gun. They were still waiting on results from the FBI lab that would hopefully tell them more about what they were dealing with.

The explosion of gunshots and the shatter of glass lifted him from his chair. Edie's scream ripped into his very heart as he raced down the hallway, Tiny barking wildly at his heels.

He ran into the bedroom where Walt had been staying to see the old man on the floor, his upper arm covered with blood and Edie on the floor at his side. The window was shattered into a hundred sparkling shards on the floor.

"Stay down," he yelled. "Margaret, call 9-1-1." He didn't wait for her response but instead raced out the front door, determined to find the shooter.

Edie would do what she could for Walt until the ambulance came, but this might be Benjamin's only chance to catch the person who seemed intent on destroying Edie and Walt.

Thank God he'd still had on his holster. He drew his gun as he left the house. The night was cold and dark and he ran around the side of the house where the shooter would have had a view of Walt's bedroom window.

He tried not to think about Walt and the blood and prayed that the old man wouldn't die before the ambulance could get here.

On this side of the house there were two structures in the distance, a shed and the barn, both perfect cover for a shooter aiming at the bedroom window.

Benjamin stayed low to the ground, grateful for the

cloudy conditions as he raced toward the shed. But before he was halfway there, he heard the sound of an engine, the tinny whine of an ATV.

He flew around the side of the shed and nearly collided with another figure. "Halt!" he yelled, his finger itching to fire his gun.

"Benjamin, it's me," Jacob said. "I heard the gunshots. He had the ATV waiting. He's gone."

Benjamin cursed soundly. "Did you see who it was?"

"No, he was too far away when I spotted him, but he was a heavyset guy."

"I've got to get back inside. He hit Walt." Benjamin was grateful to hear the sound of a siren in the distance.

"I'm going to check around out here," Jacob said as Benjamin nodded and hurried toward the house.

Dammit. Benjamin's heart raced as he went back inside. He found Edie and Walt and Margaret in the hallway. Apparently the two women had managed to drag Walt out of the bedroom.

"He got me right in the shoulder," Walt said as he saw Benjamin. The old man's face was pale as Edie pressed a towel to the wound.

"He's losing a lot of blood." She looked up at Benjamin with wild eyes.

"The ambulance is on its way." Benjamin felt helpless, filled with a rage barely contained as he crouched down next to Walt. "Hang in there, Walt. I still need to beat your ass at chess."

Walt offered him a weak grin. "Don't worry, I'm not planning on going anywhere."

At that moment the ambulance arrived along with Tom and Caleb. Caleb followed the ambulance with Edie and Margaret in tow while Benjamin remained at the house to explain the events to Tom.

He'd just finished when Jacob came in the door. Tom raised an eyebrow at the sight of his reclusive brother. "First time I've seen you out of the cabin," he said.

Jacob shrugged. "Heard the shots and knew Benjamin might be in trouble. The perp parked the ATV behind the barn. He must have walked closer to the house to fire the shots. When I was running up, I saw him heading for the ATV. But before I could get close enough to get a shot or see who it was, he was gone."

"You get a general impression…height…weight?" Tom asked.

"I'm heading to the hospital," Benjamin said before Jacob could reply. "I didn't see anything, I can't help you here," he said with frustration.

Tom nodded. "Go. Jacob and I can take care of things until you get back."

Minutes later in his truck, Benjamin's thoughts weren't on the perp, but rather on Walt and Edie. He'd let them down. He'd promised he'd keep them safe and he'd screwed up. He shouldn't have been sitting in his chair, he should have been walking the floors, checking the windows and keeping vigil.

He shouldn't be a deputy. It wasn't where he belonged. He'd known it for a long time now, but he'd been so afraid of being nothing, he'd held on to the legacy that his older brother had begun. And people had nearly died. At least he prayed they'd gotten Walt help in time.

By the time he reached the hospital he was sick with worry. He went in through the emergency room doors and immediately saw Edie and Margaret sitting side by side.

"What's going on?" he asked.

"They won't let us back there and nobody has told us anything," Edie said. Anguish was thick in her voice.

"The doctor said he'd speak to us as soon as he could," Margaret added. She reached over and patted Edie's knee. "Walt is strong and he's too onery for the devil to want him. He'll be fine." Although she said the words with a lightness in her tone, her dark eyes were filled with worry.

Benjamin shoved his hands in his pockets and leaned against the wall, anger battling with guilt inside him. "I should have done things differently," he said in frustration. "I thought the ranch would be safe. I thought if you were inside the house nothing bad would happen."

"Don't," Edie said. "Don't blame yourself for this."

"I can't help it," he replied. "It would have been different if we'd had enough manpower to station men around the ranch. I should have realized that I wasn't enough to keep you and Walt safe."

At that moment Dr. Drake came out to speak to them. Edie jumped up from her chair and stood next to Benjamin. "He's fine," Dr. Drake began. Edie sagged against Benjamin in obvious relief. "Thankfully the bullet entered and exited the fleshy part of his upper arm. We're going to give him a blood transfusion and keep him here so we can watch the wound for infection."

"I'll see that a guard is put on him during his hospitalization," Benjamin said. One way or another Tom would have to arrange for protection for the old man.

Margaret stood from the chair. "And I'll be staying with him as long as he's here," she said and raised her chin as if to argue with anyone who might protest. "Nobody's going to hurt him while I'm on duty."

"Can I see him?" Edie asked.

Dr. Drake nodded. "Go on back."

Edie started through the door and then turned to Margaret. "He'll want to see you, too."

Margaret offered her a grateful smile and together the two women disappeared behind the door.

Benjamin raked a hand down his face as Dr. Drake offered him a commiserating smile. "Bad night."

"Could have been worse," Benjamin replied. "If that bullet had hit Walt an inch lower, an inch to the left, then I'd be having a conversation with the coroner right now."

The two men turned as the door whooshed open and Tom walked in. "How's Walt?" he asked.

"A lucky man," Benjamin replied. As Dr. Drake said his goodbye and left, Benjamin looked at his older brother. "I've promised a guard here on Walt for as long as he remains in the hospital."

"Done," Tom agreed. "I'll make the arrangements."

Benjamin frowned. "There is something I don't understand. Whoever is behind this has to know that Walt and Edie are no threat to them. Why the attacks on them?"

"Jacob seems to think we're dealing with somebody who's so angry that the body parts have come to light that it's more about revenge than anything else."

"Whoever it is, he's a nasty piece of work," Benjamin replied.

"I've got several of the men checking out the ATVs in the area to see if any are still warm from riding. Walt should be safe here with a guard at the door, but what are we going to do about Edie?" Tom asked. "Maybe it's time she head back to Topeka."

"She doesn't want to go home yet. She's afraid, Tom, afraid that the person will follow her back there. With what's happened tonight, I don't feel comfortable telling her that's an unwarranted fear." Once again Benjamin raked a hand across his jaw. "I think the best thing to do is to check her into the motel for a couple days. I'll stay there with her and make sure she'd safe."

"She'll agree to that?"

Benjamin hesitated a moment and then nodded. "Yeah, she'll agree to it. What I need is for you and the others to solve this thing as soon as possible."

"Jacob is leaning on his contact in the FBI lab so hopefully we'll get some ID results from those body parts sooner rather than later. And by the way, he said to tell you that you should do whatever you need to do and he'll make sure Tiny is taken care of."

Benjamin frowned, thinking of all the logistics. "Maybe we should leave my truck here, make sure we aren't followed, and you can drop Edie and me off at the motel. That way hopefully nobody will know we're there except Brett, and he won't tell anyone if we ask him not to."

"On another note, I think we might have another missing young woman," Tom said.

Benjamin wouldn't have thought his tension level could climb any higher, but this news sent it through the roof. "Who?"

"Suzy Bakersfield. Her boyfriend called a little while ago and said she should have been home from work an hour ago. I've got Dan Walker checking it out."

Suzy Bakersfield was a twenty-four-year-old who worked as a waitress at Harley's, a rough-and-tumble bar at the edge of town. "Let's hope she just decided to go home with somebody else and didn't want her boyfriend to know." Benjamin shoved his hands in his pockets and stared at his brother. "You think these missing women are tied to whatever else is going on?"

Tom's frown deepened and for a moment he looked older than his thirty-six years. "I don't know what in the hell is going on in this town. It's impossible to know if the two are related until we have more information. All I really know is that I have a terrible feeling that things are going to get much worse before they get better."

Benjamin clapped a hand on his brother's shoulder.

"We'll get through this, Tom. Just like we got through Mom and Dad's deaths, just like we got through Brittany's disappearance. We'll get through it because that's what we Grayson men do."

Tom flashed him a grateful smile as Benjamin dropped his hand back to his side. "Let me know when you're ready to take Edie to the motel. In the meantime I'm going to step outside, get on my phone and make some arrangements."

Benjamin watched him go and then sat in one of the chairs to wait for Edie. It could have been her. That bullet could have easily hit her, killed her.

How could he protect her from an unknown assailant? One who was so filled with the need for some twisted revenge that he'd stop at nothing?

Within thirty minutes Sam McCain walked through the door. His coffee-colored face offered Benjamin a smile. "You okay?"

"As okay as I'm going to get."

"Tom tagged me for the first guard duty on Walt."

"Hopefully it will be a quiet, uneventful shift for you."

"There hasn't been a quiet, uneventful moment in the past couple of days," Sam returned.

"You got that right," Benjamin replied.

As Sam left the room to find Walt, Benjamin returned to his chair. His head spun with thoughts. Who the hell was behind all this? More importantly, would he be able to keep Edie safe until the guilty were behind bars?

Chapter 9

Two things struck Edie as she left Walt's room and returned to the waiting room. The first was that she was filled with a sick adrenaline that she didn't know what to do with and the second was that she could feel a queasy guilt wafting from Benjamin.

He rose from his chair as she entered. "Is he all right?" he asked.

She nodded. "He's going to be just fine, and I have a feeling that if he needs anything at all then Margaret will make sure he has it. What happens now?"

"I've made arrangements for Tom to take us to the motel. We can stay there for a couple days without anyone knowing we're there. I'm confident by then we'll have all this figured out." His gaze held hers, as if anticipating an argument. "Or maybe the best thing for you to do is to find another hotel in a different town."

She considered her options. The idea of running away from danger was definitely appealing, but she didn't want to leave Poppy. Besides, she had a terrible fear that no matter where she tried to hide, she'd eventually be found by the madman who was after her.

"I can't go," she finally said. "I don't want to leave Poppy. At least here I know you have my back."

He frowned. "Yeah, a lot of good that did you tonight."

She grabbed his hand in hers. "Don't do that, Benjamin. Don't blame yourself for what happened. There was no way you could have anticipated this happening." She released his hand. "Let's just get to the motel and get some sleep."

The adrenaline that had filled her from the moment the window had exploded and Poppy had fallen to the floor began to ebb a bit.

She knew she should be terrified that there was obviously somebody who was determined to kill her or Poppy or both of them. She also knew that Poppy would be safe here in the hospital. Deputy Sam McCain had assured her that nobody would get into his room unless they were hospital personnel and even then they would all be scrutinized carefully.

It took nearly an hour for them to finally leave the hospital and get checked into the motel. The room was ordinary with two double beds, a small table shoved against the wall and a wardrobe holding a television.

"Brett Hatcher, the man who owns this place, will make sure that nobody knows we're here," Benjamin said once they got inside.

Edie nodded and sat on the bed nearest the door. She was exhausted and yet keyed up at the same time. Even though it was late she knew she wouldn't be able to sleep for some time.

Benjamin moved to the window and pulled the curtains tightly closed and then turned back to look at her. "Normally I'd have you sleep in the bed nearest the window so that I'd be between you and anyone who might come in that door, but with the events of tonight still fresh in my mind I don't want you anywhere near the window."

"I trust your judgment," she said.

"You shouldn't," he replied with a touch of bitterness as he sat on the bed opposite her. "I should have never put you two at the ranch without a dozen guards on the property."

"Benjamin, I know how small this town is, how many men are working for the sheriff's department. There wasn't the manpower to post guards. You can't beat yourself up about this. It certainly hasn't shaken my confidence in you."

She watched as some of the tension in his shoulders eased. "I swear to God, Edie, I'd take a bullet in the chest before I'd let anything happen to you."

The depth of his feelings for her was there on his face, shining from his eyes and tangible in the air. She felt it wrapping around her and for several agonizing seconds she forgot how to breathe, she couldn't catch her breath.

"I know," she finally managed to say and then jumped up off the bed. "I'm going to take a shower before going to sleep." She escaped into the bathroom where she leaned weakly against the wall.

She'd sworn she didn't want or need anyone in her life, but at the moment her need for Benjamin filled her up inside. She wanted him to hold her, to stroke fire into her veins, to kiss her until she was mindless with pleasure.

She wanted to believe that her need arose from the night's events, from the fact that death had come so close, but she knew the truth. This need, this want of him, had been a slow, steady burn that had been building with each and every moment she spent with him.

Turning on the water in the shower, she tried to tamp down her desire for him. Hopefully in a week or so this would all be over and she would be back in Topeka figuring out her life.

Benjamin deserved more than a temporary woman; he deserved more than her. She stepped into the hot, steamy water and welcomed the relaxing spray that slowly unkinked taut muscles.

She just needed to get into bed and go to sleep. She needed to not think about the fact that Benjamin would be in bed only three feet from her.

At least he'd gotten a room with two beds. Sharing the room for a couple days was going to be difficult enough, but if they'd had to share a bed it would have been nearly impossible.

After several minutes she turned off the water, stepped out of the tub and grabbed one of the fluffy white towels that awaited her. She dried off and then ran her fingers through her wet hair to rid it of tangles.

She hated to put on her same clothes, but had no other choice. When she finally got beneath the sheets she'd take off her jeans and sweatshirt and sleep in her bra and panties.

When she left the bathroom she found Benjamin seated where he'd been when she'd left the room, on the edge of his bed. "At the hospital Tom told me that we might have another missing woman," he said.

"Oh, no! Who is it?" She sat on her bed facing him, so close she could smell his scent, that slightly woodsy cologne that had become as familiar as the beat of her own heart.

"Her name is Suzy Bakersfield. She works as a waitress at Harley's, a bar on the edge of town. She was due home from work a couple hours ago and her boyfriend called when she didn't come home."

"Do you think these missing women are related to the other stuff?" she asked.

He blew a deep sigh. "I don't know. I asked Tom the same question, but we just don't know enough at this point. What worries me is that if they aren't related, then we have two separate criminal issues going on here in Black Rock. I figure now isn't the time to talk to my brother about quitting."

Edie looked at him in surprise. "You're really thinking about it? I hope your decision doesn't have anything to do with what happened tonight."

His eyes were dark as he held her gaze. "It's something I've been thinking about for a long time, but I've been afraid."

"Afraid?" She couldn't imagine a man like Benjamin being afraid of anything.

Once again he released a sigh and averted his gaze from hers. Instead he stared at the wall just to the left of her, a frown racing across his forehead. "I've wanted to ranch full-time for a while now, but I've been scared of what people might think, about what might lie beneath my badge."

"I don't understand," she replied.

"The badge gives me respect in this town. People know they can depend on me and they like me. I've been afraid that if I take off the badge, then I'd be nothing. I'd lose the respect of my friends and neighbors."

"Oh, Benjamin, people like and respect you because you're a good man with a good heart. You're warm and friendly and solid and any respect you've earned has nothing to do with your badge," she exclaimed.

He offered her a smile. "You're the reason why I've decided when these cases are finished, then I'm handing in my badge."

"Me?" She looked at him in surprise. "What did I do?"

His eyes took on a new warmth, a sweet depth that was intoxicating. "I know you're afraid and yet you've handled all this with such courage and grace. Fear isn't stopping you from doing whatever it is you feel you need to do. I figure if you can do that, then so can I."

This time it was she who broke eye contact. "You should do whatever it is that makes you happy, Benjamin. Happiness is so fleeting and when it stands in front of you, you should embrace it with all of your being."

She got up from the bed and pulled down the spread. She needed to stop the conversation, needed to distance herself from him. She didn't want him to admire her. She didn't want him to look at her with his soulful eyes that made her want to fall into his arms and somehow believe that happiness might be hers to embrace.

He seemed to sense her need for distance. "I think I'll take a fast shower," he said as he got up from the bed.

"I'm sure I'll be asleep when you get out so I'll just say good-night now," she replied. She turned off the lamp next to the bed, plunging the room into darkness other than the light spilling in from the bathroom.

He hesitated at the doorway of the bathroom, as if he wanted to say something more to her. She refused to look at him again, afraid that somehow, someway, he'd break down her defenses. He finally murmured a good-night and retreated into the bathroom.

She quickly took off her jeans and T-shirt and got into her bed. With the covers pulled up around her neck, she squeezed her eyes tightly closed and tried not to think about the look she'd seen in Benjamin's eyes.

As she lay in the darkness of the room, she recognized

what she felt from him, what she saw whenever he looked at her.

Love. And it made her realize that no other man had ever looked at her in that way, that she'd never truly been loved by a man before.

She'd thought Greg loved her and she'd believed she loved him. But looking back on that relationship, she recognized it had been emotional need that had driven her into his arms and financial need that had driven him into hers.

In all her relationships before, the missing element had been the kind of love she saw shining from Benjamin's eyes whenever he looked at her.

He'd said he wished he'd met her before Greg and she wished the same. Perhaps then her heart would have been opened to taking what he seemed to be offering her, open to giving back to him tenfold.

But it was too late.

He was too late.

Still, a little part of her wondered what it would be like to make love with somebody who truly loved her?

Benjamin stood beneath the spray of the shower until it began to cool. Somewhere in the span of the events of the past couple days he'd made his decision to turn in his badge. He wouldn't do it now, with Tom so overloaded by what was happening, but within the next few months he would follow his heart and become a full-time rancher.

When he thought about spending all his days and

nights at the ranch in all his imaginings, Edie was there at his side.

He could easily see himself walking up the lane from the pasture and her seated on the front porch waiting for him to return. It was easy to imagine the two of them on horseback, her laughter riding the fresh-scented air and her eyes sparkling with that light that made him weak in the knees.

He'd never felt this way about a woman before, suspected he would never feel this depth of love again. She was a burn in his soul, a song in his heart and he knew that no matter what happened between them, she'd transformed him as a man forever.

He stepped out of the shower and quickly dried off, his head still filled with thoughts of Edie. She'd shown him that he was capable of love, of great passion for a woman. He'd begun to believe that it wasn't in his character to feel those emotions. She made him feel more alive than he had in all his years of life.

He didn't bother putting his shirt back on but pulled on his briefs and his jeans and left the bathroom. The room was dark and silent and he thought she must already be asleep.

He shucked his jeans to the floor and placed his gun on the nightstand, then slid in beneath the sheets that smelled faintly of bleach and fabric softener.

He was exhausted but he instinctively knew that sleep was a long time coming. His mind whirled not only with the shooting of Walt, but also the possibility that another woman had gone missing.

Hopefully Suzy Bakersfield had just gone off with a girlfriend and hadn't checked her plans with her boyfriend. That she was alive and well and would have some explaining to do when she eventually returned home.

But he couldn't dismiss the sick feeling that she was just like Brittany, just like Jennifer Hightower, and she'd somehow disappeared into thin air.

As always thoughts of his missing sister caused a deep grief to rip through his heart. The idea of never seeing her smile again, never hearing her babble about men and work and life, left a hole inside him that he knew would never completely be filled.

"Benjamin, are you asleep?" Edie's voice whispered across the darkness of the room.

"No."

"Me, either," she said and released a deep sigh.

"Things on your mind? Do you need to talk?" He rolled over on his side to face her direction.

She was silent for a long moment. "I'm reconsidering this celibacy thing."

Every muscle in his body froze. He was afraid to speak, afraid to hope what her words might mean. He realized she was waiting for some sort of a response from him. "Oh, really?" he finally managed to utter. "What's changed your mind?"

"You."

He heard her change positions and knew that she'd turned to face his direction. "How did I change your mind?" he asked. His breath was painful in his chest as he tried not to anticipate what might happen next.

"I don't know, you just did," she said with a hint of frustration in her voice. "I want you, Benjamin. I want you to make love to me."

Joy leaped into his heart, but it was a joy tempered with caution. "Edie, I don't want a bullet through the window to force you to make a decision you'll regret later." As much as he wanted her, he didn't want to be just another mistake in her life.

"As long as you'd understand that it's a one-shot deal, that there are no promises or strings attached, then I wouldn't regret it."

Funny, most men would have jumped at the chance for sex with no strings, no commitments, but Benjamin had hoped for more, had desperately wanted more from her.

"Benjamin?" Her whisper held both a wealth of longing and more than a hint of self-consciousness.

He'd take what he could get of her, he thought as he threw back the sheet and got up and then grabbed his wallet from the nightstand. He had a condom tucked inside it, compliments of his brother Caleb who insisted the Grayson men were always prepared.

He was surprised to discover his fingers trembling slightly as he pulled the condom out and placed it on the nightstand next to her bed.

He hesitated, wishing there was some illumination in the room so he could see her face. "Edie, are you sure?"

Her hand reached out and touched his, then her fingers twined with his and she tugged him into her bed. As he got beneath the sheets he felt nervous, excited and as if he were about to make love for the very first time.

He pulled her into his embrace and she came willingly, eagerly. She was all heat and soft curves against him as she hid her face in the crook of his neck.

He stroked his hands up the length of her back, unsurprised that her skin was as silky as he'd imagined. He wanted to say words of love, wanted her to know just how much he cared about her, but he knew that would only drive her away.

She needed this not to matter and so he told himself it didn't, that it was just a hookup for mutual sexual pleasure and nothing more.

Still, when he found her lips with his he drank of her, his heart filling with her taste, the clean soapy scent of her and the warmth that raced through his veins.

"I knew you'd feel so good," she said as he left her mouth and rained kisses down the side of her jaw. She released a small moan as he found a sensitive place just below her ear.

"And I knew the same about you," he murmured.

Her arms tightened around him and she stroked her fingers down his back, increasing the flame that threatened to consume him.

His hunger for her wanted to move fast, to rip the panties and bra from her body and take her with hard, fast strokes. He wanted to possess her in a way she'd never been possessed before, in a way that would make her cling to him now and forever.

But his need was tempered with the desire to go slow, to savor each and every moment that he held her in his arms for he knew this moment probably wouldn't happen again.

He captured her mouth again, their tongues swirling together in a deeply intimate kiss. At the same time his hands moved to her bra fastener. He hesitated, waiting to make sure she wouldn't suddenly protest. When she didn't he unfastened the whisper of fabric.

She shrugged it off and tossed it to the end of the bed, then went back into his arms. His heart banged against his chest at the feel of her warm breasts against him.

She fit neatly against him, as if they were made to fit together. She leaned back slightly and stroked a hand down his chest. "So strong," she murmured and pressed her lips against his collarbone.

He wasn't strong, not where she was concerned. He felt weak and vulnerable and needy as he captured her breasts with his hands. "So beautiful," he whispered. "You make me weak, Edie."

"I don't want you weak right now. I want you strong and powerful."

Her words merely increased his raging need of her. He bent his head and took the tip of one of her nipples in his mouth, enjoying the gasp of pleasure that escaped her.

Her nipple hardened and extended in his mouth as she tangled her fingers in his hair and moaned. She pressed her body into his and he knew she had to realize that he was fully aroused.

Rather than warding her off, his erection seemed to intensify her desire. She grabbed his buttocks, her fingers burning through the thin cotton of his briefs.

He ran a hand down the flat of her belly and slid it under the slick silk of her panties. Hot and damp, she arched up to meet his touch.

A sudden impatience snapped through him. He wanted to be naked and he wanted her naked. He tugged at her panties to remove them and she aided him by lifting her hips.

He then took off his own and pulled her back into his arms, reveling in the feel of bare skin against skin.

Again he touched her damp heat and she caught her breath and then moaned his name. His heart expanded with love for her. Wanting to be the best lover she'd ever had, he increased the pressure of his touch, felt the rising tide of sensation inside her.

He ran his lips across her cheek, down the length of her neck and moaned in pleasure as she reached her climax. She shuddered and cried out his name once more as she went limp.

She didn't stay that way for long. As she reached out and encircled his hard length with her hand, it was his turn to gasp in pleasure.

Control it. He was definitely going to lose control if she continued to touch him that way. He slid away from her and reached for the condom on the nightstand, mentally thanking his little brother for insisting that he be prepared for the unexpected.

When he was ready he crouched over her and framed

her face with his hands. He could easily imagine how her eyes looked at the moment, emerald and glowing with fire. He kissed her lips, her cheek and then her forehead as he slowly eased into her.

Engulfed in exquisite pleasure, he whispered her name again and again and began to stroke in and out of her sweet heat. She gripped his buttocks, drawing him in deep with each thrust.

Lost. He was lost in her and he never wanted to be found. But all too quickly he felt the rise of a tidal wave building up inside him, sweeping him toward completion.

When it came, he took her mouth with his in a kiss that held all the emotions he had inside. And when it was over he slumped to the side of her in awe.

Benjamin had enjoyed sex plenty of times in his life, but never with the kind of love he felt for this woman. His Edie.

No, not his. The deal was that this meant nothing to her. Just physical release without any strings. She'd made it clear in a hundred different ways that she had no intention of loving him back.

But that didn't mean he couldn't try to break through her defenses and win her heart. He rolled over and kissed her, then slid out of bed. "I'll be right back," he said and went into the bathroom.

He washed up and then stared at his reflection in the mirror. He'd never seen her coming. He'd had no way to prepare himself for the tremendous emotion Edie evoked inside him. He'd been utterly helpless to stop himself from loving her.

And he was equally helpless to stop her from leaving him. The sad truth was the people you loved didn't always love you back. But he wouldn't stop trying to win her love until she left town. He'd hold her through the nights, keep her safe and as happy as possible during the days and maybe, just maybe, his love would win.

He turned out the light and left the bathroom. "Good night, Benjamin," she said as he stepped back into the room. Any thought he had of holding her through the night vanished as he realized she didn't want him in her bed again.

"Good night," he replied and crawled beneath the covers on his own bed. He smelled of her and he wanted to keep that scent in his head forever. But, he knew that eventually this case would be solved and just like Brittany, she'd be gone from him forever.

"You have to stop crying," Brittany said to Jennifer Hightower. "You're going to make yourself sick."

"What difference does it make," Jennifer cried. "He's going to kill us anyway."

Brittany snaked her fingers through the bars that separated the two women and attempted to stroke her hair. Jennifer had been crying since their captor had brought in Suzy Bakersfield about an hour ago. Suzy was now unconscious on a cot in the third cell of five in what appeared to be an old, converted barn or shedlike structure.

Brittany had lost count of the days she'd been held captive, although she thought Jennifer had been with her for a couple weeks. She knew from experience that Suzy would remain unconscious for the rest of the night and would awaken sometime tomorrow to horror.

Horror had become an intimate companion to Brittany. When she'd initially awakened in the small cell, she'd screamed herself hoarse and had desperately tried to find a way out, but there was none. The structure was sound, with no apparent weaknesses that could be exploited. Each cell had a cot and a toilet and nothing else that could be used as a weapon or for escape.

They were usually fed a small meal once a day by their captor, but several times there had been nothing for two or three days. Each time he came in, Brittany tried her best to identify him, but he always wore a hat and a ski mask that made it impossible. His voice sounded vaguely familiar but no matter how she racked her brain she couldn't place it.

"Jenny, you didn't eat the food he brought. You need to stop crying and eat. We have to keep up our strength so that if an opportunity arises we can escape." Brittany pulled her hand back from Jenny's head and instead gripped the metal bars that separated the two.

"You can't give up hope," Brittany said, even though she struggled with that, as well.

"There is no hope," Jenny sobbed. She raised her head and looked at Brittany, her eyes swollen nearly shut and her skin splotchy from her tears.

"There's always hope," Brittany said fervently. "As long as we're alive, there's hope."

Brittany had to believe that, she had to believe that somehow her brothers would find them before the last two cells were filled with women, for it was then that she knew their captor intended to begin his game—and the game meant death to them all.

Chapter 10

It was impossible to tell what time it was when Edie awakened the next morning. She knew that Benjamin was already awake. She could hear him in the bathroom and apparently he was talking to somebody on his cell phone.

She'd known making love with him was a mistake, albeit a glorious mistake. Her body still tingled with the memory of his every touch, his every kiss, and there was no way to deny that he was in her heart as deeply as anyone ever had been.

She'd made glorious love with him and she now could no longer deny her love for him and yet really nothing had changed. She couldn't magically undo her past and she refused to let down her guard.

Benjamin was a good man who deserved a good

woman. The charm around her neck suddenly felt as if it burned her skin. She reached up and grabbed it in her hand and for a moment allowed the pain to race through her.

The charm wasn't a symbol of her mother's death, but rather the death of her baby, the daughter who had died without drawing a breath.

A medical mystery, the doctor had said with sympathy in his eyes. A tragedy, the nurse had replied as she'd gently wrapped the perfectly formed infant in a pink blanket.

But Edie had known better. It had been her fault. Somehow she'd done something wrong. She'd been so stressed over the bills and Greg's abandonment. She knew in her heart of hearts it was all her fault.

"They'll be other babies," the doctor had said when he'd signed her release papers. "You're young and healthy and I'm sure there are healthy babies in your future."

But he'd been wrong. The day Edie had buried the daughter she'd named Mary, she'd buried any hope she had, any expectation she might entertain for happiness.

Before the grief could completely overwhelm her, she released the charm and drew a deep breath. This was her secret. Oh, the few friends she had in Topeka knew that she'd lost her baby, but after the birth she'd distanced herself from them all, unable to stand the sympathy in their eyes, the platitudes that rolled so easily off their tongues.

She'd just wanted to be alone with her grief, and there was a part of her that still felt that way. She reached over and turned on the lamp on the nightstand, then got out of bed and quickly pulled on the clothes she'd taken off the night before. She felt better prepared to face the day, to face Benjamin, dressed.

When the door to the bathroom opened, she tensed. The last thing she wanted was a morning after, a rehash of the mistake she'd made the night before.

"Oh, good. You're awake," he said as he came into the room. He walked over to the window and opened the heavy outer curtains, leaving the gauzy inner curtains in place. Sunshine poured in but it was impossible to see out or into the room.

"I was just talking to Tom. He called to tell me the lab report came in." He sat on the edge of the bed and smiled at her and in his eyes, in the warmth of that smile, she saw the memories of their lovemaking.

"Did the results tell you anything about the person responsible?"

"First of all, the good news is that nothing was radioactive. In mixing some of the chemicals a reaction occurred that created the fluorescent glow, but nothing was radioactive. The bulk of the chemicals were ones used almost exclusively by taxidermists, so Tom was on his way to the taxidermy shop to speak to Jeff Hudson and his son, Jeffrey Allen."

"You think they're responsible for this?" she asked. She didn't want to look at him, didn't want to remember the feel of his warm lips against hers, the stroke of his hands across her naked body.

"I think it's a good lead," he replied. "Maybe it won't be long before this is all over." He stood. "In the meantime I called Brett and he's going to bring us some coffee and breakfast in a few minutes."

"Room service? I didn't know motels offered that."

He smiled again, the warm, wonderful grin that made her want to run into his arms, or run as far away from him as possible.

"We've used the motel off and on over the years when we've needed to stash somebody away. Brett is very accommodating when that happens."

As if to punctuate his sentence, there was a knock on the door. Instantly tension replaced Benjamin's warm smile as he drew his gun from his shoulder holster and motioned her into the bathroom.

He peered out the window and instantly relaxed. "It's okay. It's Brett."

He unchained and unlocked the door to admit the older man who carried with him a large shopping bag. He nodded at Edie and walked over to the small table. "Got you some coffee and egg muffins and a couple of sweet rolls," he said.

"Thanks, Brett, we appreciate it," Benjamin replied.

"No problem. Just call the office when you need something else and I'll be happy to do food runs for you." With another nod to Edie he left the room.

Benjamin locked the door behind him as Edie began

to unload the food. Maybe she'd feel better after a cup of coffee. A caffeine rush would surely banish her desire to be back in Benjamin's arms.

They sat at the small table and ate, talking little until the food was gone and they were left with the last of their coffee.

"The good news for the town is that the wooded area where the body parts were found wasn't contaminated and won't require an expensive cleanup," he said. "Something like that could bankrupt a small town like Black Rock."

"That is good news for you," she replied.

"And we'll have good news for you soon," he said softly. "This is going to be over and the person who attacked you will be behind bars."

"From your lips to God's ears." She took a sip of coffee and broke off eye contact with him. It was there again in his eyes, a soft vulnerability, a sweet longing that scared her.

"Edie." The longing she'd seen in his eyes was now in his voice.

She closed her eyes, refusing to look at him. "Benjamin, don't." She was afraid of what he was about to say, didn't want to hear whatever he thought might be in his heart.

"I have to," he said, obviously knowing exactly what she meant. "My lack of real passion used to worry me. I've watched two of my brothers fall in love. I saw the passion in their eyes, heard it in their voices whenever they saw or talked about their women. I thought something was missing inside me. I'd never felt that for any woman I'd dated, until now. Until you."

There it was, out on the table, the one thing she didn't want to hear from him, the last thing she'd wanted to hear. She forced herself to look at him and the emotion in his eyes was raw and open for her to see.

"I love you, Edie. I love you passionately, desperately and I want you to stay here in Black Rock with me. I want you in my life today and forever."

It was exactly what she'd feared. She was going to be his first heartbreak and she hated it; she hated herself for not being the woman he needed in his life.

"Benjamin, you're just feeling that way because of last night," she said. "I'll admit, the sex was great. We obviously have a physical chemistry, but I've told you all along, I'm not looking for a relationship."

"Sometimes when you aren't looking for love it finds you anyway," he countered. He reached across the table for her hand, but she pulled away, not wanting his touch, which would simply make things more difficult. "Edie, I'm a simple man, but I believe you love me. I see it when you look at me, I tasted it in your kisses last night. I've had sex with women before, but last night we made love, both of us together."

She desperately sought the words to deny her own feelings for him, but they refused to rise to her lips. Once again she looked down at the top of the table, finding it impossible to look into his eyes without drowning in his feelings for her.

"It doesn't matter. Don't you see?" She got up from

the table and stepped away from him. "It doesn't matter what you feel, and it doesn't matter what I feel. I'm still going back to Topeka and living my life alone."

A sudden grief clawed up her throat, burned in her eyes, the grief of knowing she was turning her back on love and the darker, deeper grief of overwhelming loss.

She gripped the back of the chair, her knuckles white as she fought for control. But the fight was in vain. Tears began to run down her cheeks as an agonizing pain ripped through her. "Please, Benjamin, leave it alone," she managed to gasp. "I'm not the kind of woman you want. You deserve better than me."

She looked around wildly, needing to escape not only from him, but also from her own dark thoughts, from the incredible pain that threatened to shatter her into pieces.

He got up from his chair and took her by the shoulders, forcing her to look up at him. "What are you talking about, Edie? You are the woman I want and we both deserve to be happy together. I'll ranch full-time and you can do whatever makes you happy as long as each morning I wake up to see your face and each night I fall asleep with the sound of your breathing next to me."

He moved his hand to her cheek and softly stroked there. "We'll build a life together. We'll laugh and we'll love. Each night when the weather is nice, we'll sit on the front porch and watch the horses play as the sun sets. It will be a wonderful life, Edie, if only you'll share it with me."

It was magical picture he painted with his words, one she wanted to step into and embrace and she felt her resolve fading, her defenses crumbling.

"Come on, Edie. You know you love me. Let's raise cattle and children together."

Of all the things he might have said, this was the one thing that exploded apart the picture of happily-ever-after, and her weeping began in earnest.

She didn't want to tell him. She'd never wanted to tell anyone. But she was certain it was the one thing that would turn him away in revulsion, the one thing that would change his mind about loving her.

And ultimately that would make it so much easier on her. If he'd just stop loving her. Then perhaps she wouldn't want him as desperately, as frantically as she did.

"Talk to me, Edie. Why are you crying?" He used his thumbs to wipe at the tears on her cheeks.

She wasn't sure what she was crying for, if it was because she had every intention of walking away from this wonderful man or if she cried for the child who had never been, the sweet baby daughter she'd lost.

He attempted to pull her into his arms, but she whirled away from him, wild with her grief. She headed for the bathroom, needing the privacy, but before she went inside she turned back to face him.

"You don't know me, Benjamin. You don't know what I've done."

"Then tell me. I know nothing you can say will

change the way I feel about you. Nothing that you have done will make me not love you."

He was like a shimmering mirage in the veil of her tears, a mirage that looked like love but she knew if she let him close enough it would disappear.

"I killed my baby, Benjamin. That's what I did." She watched his eyes widen and saw the shock that swept over his features just before she escaped into the bathroom and locked the door.

Benjamin felt as if he'd been sucker punched in the gut. Of all the things he'd anticipated she might have said, there was no way he could have anticipated this.

The one thing he knew was that there was no way Edie could intentionally harm anyone, especially her own baby. He stared at the closed bathroom door, the sound of her weeping drifting through the door.

She'd hit him like a speeding, out-of-control driver and then had left before checking for damage or explaining why she'd been reckless in the first place.

After everything they'd been through he deserved more from her. He knocked on the bathroom door. "Edie," he said, steeling his heart against the sound of her crying. He tried the doorknob, unsurprised to find it locked. "Edie, come out here and talk to me. I haven't asked you for much, but you owe me an explanation."

Her sobs were gut-wrenching. He heard her gasping for air, hiccupping as they began to subside. He remained standing outside the door until there was finally silence on the other side.

"Edie, please talk to me," he finally said. He stepped back as the doorknob turned and the door opened. The ravages of pain were on her splotchy face, in her red-rimmed eyes, and he wanted nothing more than to take her into his arms.

She didn't meet his gaze as she moved past him and sat on the edge of his bed. She stared down at the carpet beneath her feet, her shoulders slumped forward in utter defeat.

"I was almost seven months pregnant when Greg abandoned me." Her voice was flat, as if she'd forgotten all her emotions in the bathroom. "I was reeling with the financial mess he'd left me, still grieving for my mother and wondering how I was going to deal with being a single parent."

He wanted to sit next to her, wanted to pull her into his arms and tell her everything was going to be okay, but he sensed her need to do this alone, to tell her story without the comfort he might offer her.

"For the first couple weeks after he left and the creditors were calling me, I did nothing but cry." She laced her fingers together in her lap, the white knuckles letting him know how difficult it was for her to talk.

"I finally quit crying and decided I was going to be just fine. I'd be a terrific mother and I was strong enough to do it all alone." She raised her head to look at him and in her eyes he saw a woman's grief, a mother's despair.

"Everything seemed normal. I went into labor a week before my due day and got to the hospital. Halfway through the delivery I knew something was wrong. The atmosphere in the room changed and nobody was smiling or joking anymore. Eventually she arrived, a beautiful baby girl who was stillborn."

He could no longer stay away from her. He sat next to her but when he attempted to pull her into his embrace, she jerked away.

"Edie, I'm so sorry for you. I'm so sorry for your loss." His heart ached for her and he wished there was some way he could take away her pain, banish the haunting that darkened her eyes. "What did the doctor say?"

She released a bitter laugh. "That these things happen, that it was a tragic medical mystery that sometimes occurs."

"Edie, you didn't do anything wrong. Sometimes bad things happen for no reason, but that doesn't mean you should blame yourself, that you should punish yourself for the rest of your life."

She jumped up from the bed, her entire body trembling. "But I did do something wrong. In those two weeks that I was so broken, there was a night I thought for just a minute that everything would be so much easier if I wasn't pregnant. I was big and fat and uncomfortable. Don't you see, Benjamin, I wished the baby away and she was gone."

He got up off the bed and pulled her against his chest. She fought him, trying to get away, but he held tight until she collapsed against him as she cried uncontrollably.

He now understood the shadows he'd sometimes

seen in her eyes and the significance of the charm she wore around her neck. What he didn't know was how to take away the misplaced guilt she felt, how to make her understand that to deny herself happiness for the rest of her life wasn't the answer. He simply held her tight, waiting for her storm of tears to pass.

Eventually she stopped crying and simply remained exhausted in his arms. He led her back to the bed and together they sat, his arm still around her shoulder.

For several long minutes neither of them spoke. Her heartbreak hung thick and palpable in the air. He stroked her shoulder although he knew she was beyond the place where physical connection might comfort her.

He drew a deep breath. "The day before Brittany disappeared I had a fight with her. As usual she was late to work and I'd had to cover some of her shift. I was ticked and I told her that there were times my life sure would be less complicated if she'd just get out of it for a while."

He paused to draw another breath, emotion thick in the back of his throat.

Edie was as still as a statue against his side. "What did she say?" she finally asked.

"She laughed and patted my cheek and told me not to be such a grumpy bear. It was the last time I talked to her. Am I to believe that in that moment of anger I somehow made her disappear for good?"

"Of course not."

"Then why would you believe that a moment's

thought had the power to make sure your baby didn't live?"

She didn't answer. Her head remained bowed and her body felt boneless against him and he knew that he hadn't broken through to her.

"Edie, don't throw your life away because of a tragedy. You deserve to be happy, and if it's not with me, then open up your heart to somebody else."

She finally raised her head to look at him and in her eyes he saw the strength of her defenses back in place. She moved away from him and stood, her back rigid and her mouth pressed together in a grim line.

"I'm not strong like you, Benjamin. I can't forget what happened, what I lost." She reached up and touched the charm that hung around her neck.

"I don't expect you to forget," he countered. "Your daughter was a part of you, a part of your heart for nine months. You don't forget those you love and lose. You remember them and sometimes you ache for them, but life goes on and the only way to truly honor their memory is to be happy."

A panic welled up inside him as her walls climbed higher. He was going to lose her before he'd ever really had her. "Edie, for God's sake, let me in. Let me show you happiness and love."

For just a brief moment her eyes shimmered with the love he knew was deep in her heart for him. Hope filled him, but was quickly dashed as she shook her head and the emotion in her eyes vanished.

"I'm sorry, Benjamin, but when this is all over I'm

going back to Topeka. I don't need love in my life. I don't want it. I just want to live the rest of my life alone, without risk."

Once again she headed for the bathroom and disappeared inside. And this time Benjamin didn't go after her.

There was nothing more he could say, nothing more he could do, and for the first time in his life, Benjamin knew the pain of heartbreak.

Chapter 11

Edie would have liked to hide out in the bathroom forever. At least in here she didn't have to look at Benjamin, didn't have to see the love light in his eyes.

It hurt. Her love for him ached in her chest. She'd never wanted anything more in her life than a future with him, a chance to grow old with him at her side.

But she was afraid to love again, afraid to seek happiness. She couldn't forgive herself and she didn't trust that his love wasn't just some illusion to torment her.

She took a shower and lingered after dressing. She didn't want to go back inside the room and see the pain she'd inflicted on him.

She'd never wanted to break his heart. He was such a good man, as solid as the day was long and with a tenderness that was a gift to anyone who knew him.

For a moment if she closed her eyes and let herself go, she could see a future with him, she could hear the days of laughter, feel the love that would fill her world.

The moment was shattered by his knock on the door. "Edie, Tom just called. It's over. Jeffrey Allen confessed to everything."

She sagged against the door. Over. It was all over. Now there was nothing to keep her from going back to her lonely life. She straightened and opened the door. "Good, let's get the hell out of here so I can go home."

"Tom and Caleb are on their way to bring me my truck," he replied. "They should be out front in a few minutes."

"If you don't mind, I'd like to stop by the hospital on the way to the ranch. I need to tell Poppy and Margaret goodbye before I leave."

"You're leaving today?" He looked at her in surprise.

She nodded. "As soon as I get my things at your place I'll be on the road."

"That breakfast we had earlier left me hungry. Come to the café with me and eat a good lunch before you take off. I'll tell you everything Tom told me when he called."

"Only on one condition," she said. "That you don't try to talk me into staying."

The smile he gave her was a weary one with a touch of disillusionment. "I gave it my best shot, Edie. The ball is in your court. I won't try to talk you into anything."

An hour later they were seated at a table in the café.

She'd said her painful goodbyes to Poppy and Margaret and in her mind she was halfway out of town already. She'd only agreed to this meal because she had a long drive ahead of her and had to eat something before taking off. Besides, she was curious about the crime that had kept her in town, the man who had beaten Poppy and terrorized her.

"According to what Tom told me, Jeffrey decided to dabble in a little chemistry and see if he could come up with a way to better preserve flesh," Benjamin said after they'd placed their orders with the waitress.

"Apparently he was hoping to come up with some kind of cream that would work on human flesh, a beauty product that would take the world by storm."

"And so he stole body parts from the cemetery?" she asked.

Benjamin nodded. "That's what he confessed to. From what Tom said, Jeffrey believed that somehow he'd created a radioactive reaction in his experiments, hence the hazmat suit to dispose of the botched batch."

"So, why did he go after me and Poppy? He had to know that we couldn't identify him."

"Interestingly enough, Tom said those two things were what he was most reluctant to admit to. When he did, it was just like we suspected, sheer anger that drove him to attack the two of you. If he'd been successful in his experiments he would have eventually become a very wealthy man. Beauty is a big business these days and he thought he was going to discover a fountain of youth, something that would keep skin from aging."

Edie fought back a shiver as she remembered hiding in the closet while Jeffrey had banged on the door and threatened her.

"You okay?" he asked as if he sensed the fear that suddenly crawled up her back.

"I'm fine, just glad this is all over and I can go back home without looking over my shoulder."

At that moment their orders arrived. Their meal was interrupted several times by people stopping by their table to ask about Walt or talk about Jeffrey's arrest.

Benjamin introduced her to Larry Norwood, the town vet, and to Hugh Randolf, who owned the feed store. She met Karen Patterson, who worked at the bank, and Lisa Rogers, who was a beautician.

Each and every person greeted her with open friendliness and sent home the fact that if she'd chosen differently, Black Rock would have been a wonderful place to call home.

They were just leaving the café when at the door they met a big guy in overalls and a red flannel shirt. Benjamin introduced him as Josh Willoughby, the groundskeeper at the cemetery.

"Hope you're planning on staying in town," he said to Edie. "I know Walt would love having you around."

"Actually, I'm on my way out of town in just a little while," Edie replied. "This was just a visit gone crazy."

Josh smiled. "Seems to me the only one who went crazy is Jeffrey." He looked at Benjamin. "I guess we've solved the mystery of the lights I thought I saw once in a while at the cemetery. Must have been Jeffrey skulking around the newest graves."

"Must have been," Benjamin agreed. "At least this particular issue has been solved."

"Yeah, now all you have to do is figure out what happened to those missing girls," Josh replied.

Edie felt the weight of concern in Benjamin as he released a deep sigh. "Yeah, we definitely need a break where the disappearances are concerned."

Goodbyes were said and then Edie and Benjamin got back into his truck and headed for the ranch. They were both silent for part of the ride. It wasn't a comfortable silence but rather one filled with tension.

Telling him goodbye was going to rip out her heart, but she was determined not to change her course, not to alter her future.

"So, what are your plans when you get back to Topeka?" he finally asked, breaking the miserable silence.

"Find a job, find a new place to live," she replied. "Those are my two immediate concerns."

"You'll let somebody here know where you move? We might need you to come back when this goes to trial."

"You have my cell phone number. That won't change, so you can get hold of me if you need to." As the entrance to the ranch came into view she steeled her heart against a sense of homecoming.

It felt like home. It looked like home, but she reminded herself it was just an illusion. Her grandmother had always cautioned her to love smart, but she'd already made the choice not to love at all. And that was the smartest choice of all.

When they got inside she went to the bedroom where she'd stayed and began to pack her bags while Benjamin headed for the kitchen. She was grateful he didn't hover near her as she placed the few articles of clothing she'd brought back into her suitcase.

She took a clean pair of jeans and a long-sleeve emerald blouse into the bathroom and quickly changed, grateful for the clean clothes after being stuck in the others for two days.

When she left the bathroom she nearly bumped into Benjamin. "I just wanted to let you know that I called Jacob and asked him to bring Tiny back. I thought you might want to say goodbye to the mutt."

A new ball of emotion swelled up in her chest at thoughts of the little dog. She nodded and walked back into the bedroom. She grabbed her suitcase but Benjamin took it from her and together they went to the living room.

At that moment Jacob came in the door, Tiny in his arms. The dog vibrated with excitement at the sight of Edie and Benjamin. As Jacob placed Tiny on the floor he ran first to Benjamin and then to Edie.

She scooped him up in her arms and hugged him as he licked the side of her neck. She smiled at Jacob, noting that the man looked rough with a whisker-darkened jaw and the darkest eyes she'd ever seen. "Thanks for bringing him here for a goodbye."

He nodded and then turned and left the house as Edie placed the dog back on the floor.

"You'll have to excuse my brother. He's not the most social creature on earth," Benjamin said.

"That's okay. Well, I guess it's time for me to get on the road." She didn't quite meet his gaze.

"Edie, if you ever need anything, if you change your mind about me…about us, I'll be here." The yearning in his voice nearly broke her.

She picked up her suitcase and overnight bag and clung tight to the handles so that she wouldn't be tempted to throw her arms around his neck and cling tightly to him. "*Thank you* seems so inadequate for what you've done for me and Poppy, but I'm so grateful, if this had to happen to us, that it happened here with you."

She looked at him then, memorizing his beautiful brown eyes, the strong, handsome features that were permanently etched in her mind. Years from now on cold lonely nights she would remember him and the expression on his face and would be comforted by the knowledge that she'd once been loved.

Together they left the house and he stood next to her car as she stowed her suitcase in the trunk. She dug her keys out of her purse, opened the driver's door and then turned back to look at him.

"Well, I guess this is goodbye." She refused to cry in front of him even though tears began to well up inside her. "I hope you do take up ranching full-time, Benjamin. You come alive when you talk about it."

He nodded, his eyes filled with a sadness it would

take her a long time to forget. "And I hope you find peace, Edie. I hope you find forgiveness for yourself, even though you did nothing to be forgiven for. Be safe, Edie, and try to find some happiness for yourself."

He stepped away from the car and she slid in behind the steering wheel and closed the door. As she started the engine, she swallowed hard against the tears that seemed determined to fall.

Refusing to look in her rearview mirror as she pulled away, she kept her focus on the road ahead. Still, by the time she reached the entrance, her vision was blurred with the tears she could no longer contain.

She believed she was doing the right thing and yet there was a tiny voice deep inside her screaming that she was making the biggest mistake of her life.

"Shut up," she muttered to the voice. Still the tears continued and she angrily swiped at them with one hand. There was nothing to cry about. This was her decision, the right decision.

If you never looked for happiness, then you were never disappointed. If you never sought love, then your heart would always remain intact. It was the safest way to live, wrapped in a cocoon of isolation.

By the time she reached the narrow stretch of highway that would lead out of town, her tears had stopped and she kept her mind focused on all the things she needed to take care of once she got back to Topeka.

She was the only car on the road so it was easy to let her mind wander. She might try the apartments down the street from her current address. She was going to miss that smile of his. She tightened her hands on the steering wheel and consciously forced thoughts of Benjamin out of her head.

She hadn't driven very far when she saw a truck approaching fast behind her. As he got on her tail he honked and then shot into the left lane to pass her.

When he got up next to her she recognized him as the man she'd met earlier at the café. Josh something, the cemetery man. He pointed at the back of her car and gestured wildly as if something was wrong.

Terrific, just what she needed…car trouble that might keep her here for another day or two. She pulled over to the side of the road and Josh pulled in behind her.

He got out of his truck as she got out of the car. "Your back tire is going flat," he said.

"Terrific, and I don't have a spare," she exclaimed. She walked toward the rear of the car and bent down to look at the tire he'd indicated. She frowned. The tire looked fine to her.

Before she could straighten up, something slammed into the top of her head. She sprawled forward to the ground, as pinpoints of light exploded in a growing darkness. Her last conscious thought was that they'd all been wrong.

It wasn't over.

Benjamin wandered the house like a lost man, Tiny at his heels. He'd been alone for most of his adult life but he'd never felt such loneliness.

He'd told Tom he was going to take off the next couple days. With Jeffrey Allen behind bars and that particular crime solved, there were plenty of deputies who could work on the disappearance of the women. He wasn't really needed.

She didn't need you. She didn't love you enough. The words whispered through his brain, bringing with them an ache he'd never felt before.

He'd held out hope until the moment her car had disappeared from his view and it was only then that the last of his hope had died.

He thought about heading to the cabin and talking to Jacob, but realized he wasn't in the mood to talk to anyone, especially Jacob, who seemed to hate life as much as he hated himself at the moment.

There was plenty of work around the ranch that he could do and maybe that was exactly what he needed— physical labor to keep his mind away from thoughts of Edie.

He wanted to make himself so exhausted that when he closed his eyes to sleep that night he wouldn't think of her warm laughter, wouldn't smell her enticing scent and wouldn't remember how she felt in his arms.

As he left the house and headed for the barn, his thoughts turned to his sister. He would always have a little bit of guilt inside him about the last conversation he'd had with Brittany, but he knew it wasn't his fault that she'd gone missing.

Just like it wasn't Edie's fault that her baby had been stillborn. He couldn't imagine the anguish of a woman who had carried and loved her baby for nine months, gone through the agony of childbirth and then ended up with nothing.

An experience like that could definitely scar a heart, but it wasn't supposed to destroy a heart. He shook his head as he opened the barn door. Edie had allowed the tragedy and her misplaced sense of guilt to define her, and there was nothing he could do to change that.

Always before he'd found peace and comfort in the barn where the air smelled like leather and hay and horse, but this time there was no peace, no solace to be found. The only scent he wanted to smell was the sweet fragrance of Edie and she was gone from him.

He pulled out his saddle, deciding to oil the leather. He didn't know how long he'd been working when his cell phone rang. He fumbled it out of his shirt pocket and answered.

"Benjamin, we've got a problem." Caleb's voice nearly vibrated with tension. "Is Edie with you?"

Tension filled him. "No, she left here about an hour ago. She was headed back to Topeka. Why?"

"Her car is out on the highway, but she's not around."

Benjamin's heart crashed to his feet. "I'll be right there." He clicked off and then hurried for the house and his keys.

He was on the road in minutes, telling himself to calm down, that there had to be a logical explanation. She had car trouble or she ran out of gas and took off walking back to town, he thought.

But she had your phone number. Why wouldn't she have called for help? Surely she would have put all personal issues aside if she'd needed help.

By the time he pulled to the curb behind her car, he was half-wild with suppositions. Both Tom and Caleb were there, their cars parked in front of Edie's vehicle.

"There's no damage to the car," Caleb said. "And the keys are in it. I started it up and the engine purred like a kitten, and the gas tank is full."

His words shattered Benjamin's hopeful speculations. His panic must have shown on his features. "There's no blood inside, no signs of a struggle," Tom said.

"There weren't any signs of a struggle in Brittany's or Jennifer's car," he said. Was it possible she'd become the latest victim to a madman who was collecting the young women of the town? "We have to find her," he said with an urgency that made him feel half-sick. He'd lost her because she didn't love him, but he couldn't imagine losing her to this kind of fate.

For the next two hours the three officials walked the area, seeking some clue that might lead to her whereabouts. Tom had people checking in town to see if anyone had seen her. During that time Benjamin's mind raced as his heart grew heavier and heavier.

What were the odds that they'd keep her safe from one madman only to have her fall prey to another? It looked as if she'd pulled the car over on her own. What or who would make her stop?

Was it possible this wasn't another disappearance,

but rather tied to the case they'd thought was closed? But Jeffrey had confessed to everything, he reminded himself.

Dammit, he'd thought she was safe, that the danger was over. He looked at Tom, who hung up his phone and shook his head. "Nobody has seen her in town."

"I want to talk to Jeffrey," Benjamin said.

Tom looked at him in surprise. "Why? He's locked up and couldn't have anything to do with this."

Benjamin frowned thoughtfully. "I know that, but I've known Jeffrey all my life and I've never seen him lose his temper, never seen him hurt a fly." His head was a jumble of thoughts, ones he should have entertained the minute Tom had told him Jeffrey had confessed.

"The beating Walt took was vicious and Edie said the man who tried to get at her in the house was filled with rage. That just doesn't sound like Jeffrey. Besides, you said he readily confessed to the experiments and illegal dumping of the body parts yet was reluctant to confess to hurting Walt and attacking Edie."

Tom raised a dark eyebrow. "Are you thinking about a partner?"

Benjamin nodded. "Maybe somebody he's trying to protect or somebody who scares him more than time in jail."

"Let's go have a talk with him," Tom replied.

As Benjamin got into his truck to drive back to town, he prayed they'd find some answers that would lead back to Edie. He prayed that it already wasn't too late for her. He prayed that she wouldn't become another missing woman, that she wouldn't just seemingly disappear off the face of the earth and he would never know what happened to her.

Chapter 12

Edie regained consciousness in pieces of confusion. She moaned as a sharp pain raged in the back of her head and then realized moaning was all she could do because her mouth was taped closed.

Panic pumped her heart in a frantic rhythm as her eyes snapped open. Her ankles were tied, as were her hands behind her back. She sat on the dirt floor of a small shed and for several agonizing seconds she couldn't remember how she'd gotten there.

Then she remembered being in the car and heading out of town when Josh the cemetery man had caused her to stop. But why had he done this? What did he want with her?

She struggled in an attempt to free her hands, but

they were bound tight and her efforts only made the ties tighter and cut off her circulation.

How long had she been unconscious? Minutes? Hours? Did anyone know she was in trouble? Was anyone even looking for her?

Benjamin. Her heart cried his name. Had Josh taken the other women, as well? Would she become just another woman in the town of Black Rock who had disappeared without a trace?

Tears welled up in her eyes, but she shoved them back, afraid that if she began to cry she'd choke. If her nose stuffed up she would suffocate. She would have laughed out loud at this thought if it were possible. Which would she prefer, suffocation by tears or death at the hands of a crazy creep?

She couldn't wait for help to come. It might never come. She needed to do something to help herself. Wildly she looked around the dim, dusty shed. There were picks and shovels leaning in the corner, but nothing that appeared sharp enough to cut the ropes that held her.

There was a machine standing nearby, bigger than a lawnmower and with a small bucket on the front. Her blood went icy cold as she realized it was probably used to dig graves.

Was that what had happened to those other women? Were their bodies under the ground, hiding in a secret grave that Josh had dug on the cemetery property?

A new panic seared through her. Maybe she could use the blade of one of the shovels to free herself, she thought. At least she could try. She attempted to scoot across the floor but instantly discovered that her hands were not only tied together behind her back but were also anchored to something that held her in place.

Frustration added to her fear as she realized there was no way she could do anything to get out of this mess. She was at the mercy of Josh and fate.

She froze, her heart nearly stopping in her chest as she heard somebody approaching. *Please, please let it be somebody here to rescue me,* she thought. *Please, let it be Benjamin or one of his lawmen brothers who walks through that door.*

The door creaked open and her heart fell as Josh walked in. She raised her chin and gave him her best stare of defiance. He laughed, an ugly sound that twisted in her guts.

"You can glare at me all you want," he said as he leaned against the door and eyed her in amusement. "But the way I see it, I've got the upper hand here and you should be begging me for your life. Not that it would do any good."

His pleasant expression morphed into one of rage as he took a step closer to her. "You stupid bitch, you and that old man of yours ruined everything!"

He began to pace just in front of her. "Jeffrey Allen was on the verge of producing a product that would have set the cosmetic industry on its ears. I was supplying Jeffrey with body parts and he'd agreed to pay me half of whatever he made."

He stopped in front of her, his eyes wild with hatred.

"You know how much they pay me for my work here in the cemetery? Next to nothing. I got to work another job just to put food on the table. I was going to be rich but you and Walt had to stick your nose into things."

He leaned down so close to her that if her mouth hadn't been bound she would have bitten his nose off. In his eyes she saw not only a deep-seated rage but also a hint of insanity.

"You screwed up my plans." His breath was sick, fetid in her face. "And the price for that is death." He straightened and walked back to the door. "After dark tonight I'm going to do a little work in the cemetery. That gives you several hours to think about what it's going to be like to be buried alive."

Horror washed over her, making her slump back against the wall as he left the shed. She wondered what time it was, how many hours she had left before darkness fell.

Her head pounded with intensity and the taste of terror filled her mouth. She should have never stopped the car. But she'd had a false sense of safety and hadn't sensed danger.

Closing her eyes, she realized what she'd heard was true. When facing death your life flashed before your eyes. She thought of those starlit nights with her grandmother and sweet loving moments with her mother.

She regretted all the time lost with her Poppy and hoped that he and Margaret would form a lasting connection that would keep them both company until their deaths.

And she thought about Mary, the daughter she'd lost, the daughter she'd loved. She'd loved her baby and had wanted her no matter how difficult it would be as a single parent.

She'd planned for Mary, had stroked her own fat belly and sung to the baby. She'd never wished Mary away. She'd been beating herself up for something that hadn't been her fault.

In this moment of facing her own death, she realized Benjamin was right. Mary's death was a tragedy, just like Benjamin's sister's disappearance. Both had been tragedies without answers, without blame.

Tears formed in her eyes once again as she realized she'd had happiness right there in her hand. All she'd had to do was reach out and grasp it, grasp him.

Benjamin. Her heart cried out his name. She'd been a fool to let fear keep her from immersing herself in his love, for not wallowing in her own love for him. And now it was too late.

Fate had given her a chance to be with a man who loved her to distraction, a man who made her happier than anyone else on the face of the earth. It had given her the possibility of other babies and beautiful sunsets and a man who would love and support her. And she'd walked away. She'd loved smart and acted stupid and now it was too late to change things.

She looked at the cracks around the door where faint

daylight appeared. How many hours until nightfall? How many hours left before she found herself in the horror of a grave?

Jeffrey Allen Hudson looked like a broken man when Tom led him into the small interrogation room. His shoulders slumped and his broad face was pale, as if some terminal disease was eating him from the inside out.

Tom placed him into a chair at the table and gestured Benjamin toward the chair opposite Jeffrey. Benjamin didn't sit.

"I don't know what you want from me," Jeffrey said. "I've already confessed to everything." He stared down at the tabletop, refusing to look at either man.

"Jeffrey, tell me about the attack on Walt Tolliver's granddaughter." Benjamin placed his hands on the table and leaned forward.

"I already told Tom I did it, so what else is there to say?" He still didn't look up. "Why don't you just leave me alone? I'll face whatever punishment I have to, but I don't have anything else to say."

"If you cooperate with us, maybe I'll put in a good word with the prosecutor," Tom said.

Jeffrey drew a deep breath and finally looked up. His eyes were filled with torment. "What do you want from me?" he asked wearily.

Benjamin ran everything over in his mind as he tamped down the urgency that screamed inside him. "I just need to know one thing. When you stabbed Edie in the leg, did you use a paring knife from Walt's kitchen or was it a pocketknife?" He ignored Tom's look of surprise.

There was no denying the look of confusion that crossed Jeffrey's features. It was there only a moment and then gone as he focused again on the top of the table. "A pocketknife," he mumbled.

Benjamin slammed his hands down on the table. Jeffrey jumped and scooted his chair back an inch. "You're lying, Jeffrey. Who are you protecting? A friend? Your father?"

"No! My dad has nothing to do with this." Jeffrey grabbed the sides of his head with his hands.

"Jeffrey, Edie is missing. Her car was found on the side of the highway and we think she's in trouble. If you know anything, you need to tell us. Jeffrey, you don't want to be a part of her getting hurt or worse." Benjamin wanted to rip Jeffrey from his seat and shake him until the truth rattled out of his teeth.

Tears formed in Jeffrey's eyes. "He told me that he'd kill my dad if I said anything." The words were a mere whisper. "He's crazy, you know. I didn't realize it until we were both in too deep. I promised him half of what I made. He thought he was going to be rich and he was so angry when it all fell apart."

"Who, Jeffrey. Tell me who," Benjamin exclaimed, his anxiety through the ceiling. But before Jeffrey could reply the answer came to Benjamin.

"It's Josh Willoughby, isn't it?" he asked.

Panic swept across Jeffrey's face and Benjamin knew

he had his answer. He looked at his brother. "You'd better send somebody with me to Josh's place, because if I find out he's harmed Edie I'm going to kill him."

He didn't wait for an answer but instead strode out of the room and out of the station. He was on the road to Josh's house when he saw Caleb's patrol car following him.

He'd meant what he'd said. If Josh had hurt Edie... or worse, Benjamin wouldn't blink twice as he beat the life out of the man.

Josh Willoughby. They all should have realized he had something to do with this. He was in charge of the burials at the cemetery. It would have been easy for him to provide Jeffrey with the body parts before the caskets were covered with dirt.

From the moment Benjamin had heard that Jeffrey had confessed, he'd found it hard to believe that he was responsible for beating Walt and attacking Edie. It was completely out of character.

It wasn't out of character for Josh. Josh was known to have a temper and he also owned an old ATV. It made sense that Jeffrey was involved on the science end of the experiments and Josh was the one who did the dirty work.

The day was slipping away, the sun sinking low in the western sky. It would be dark soon and the thought of Edie someplace out there in the dark and in danger was almost too much for him to bear.

You're probably too late, a little voice whispered in the back of his head. He tightened his grip on the steering wheel and tried to ignore the voice. He couldn't be too late for her. He couldn't be.

He'd already lost Brittany. He couldn't lose Edie. It didn't matter that she didn't want to spend her life with him. It was just important that she have a life to live.

The cemetery came into view and just after it was Josh's small house. Josh's truck was parked out front, letting Benjamin know the man was home.

Benjamin parked in front and raced to the door where he pounded with his fist. Caleb parked just behind him and hurried to join his brother.

Josh's wife, Marylou, answered the door. She was a small, mousy woman who didn't socialize and was rarely seen in town. She eyed Benjamin and Caleb with more than a bit of trepidation. "Yes?"

"We need to talk to Josh," Benjamin said.

She didn't look surprised, just weary. "He's out back."

Benjamin leaped off the porch and headed around the side of the house, his heart beating so fast he was nearly breathless. Caleb followed just behind him. "Don't do anything stupid," he said.

"Don't worry, I plan on being smart when I beat the hell out of him," Benjamin replied tersely.

They found Josh in the backyard, a hammer in hand as he worked on a rotting windowsill. "Damn house is falling apart," he said as they approached. "What are you two doing here?"

"Put down the hammer," Caleb said as he drew his gun.

"Hey, what's going on?" Josh asked.

"Where is she?" Benjamin asked as Josh slowly lowered the hammer to the ground.

He straightened back up and looked at Benjamin with confusion. "Where is who?"

Benjamin hit him in the chest hard with both his hands. "You know who I'm talking about. Where is Edie?"

Josh stumbled back a step, his face flushing with color. "Hey, man, what's the matter with you? I don't know what you're talking about."

A white-hot rage flew through Benjamin. He slammed Josh on the chin with his fist. "We can do this the easy way or we can do it the hard way," Benjamin said.

Josh grabbed his jaw. "What's wrong with you? You're crazy, man." He looked at Caleb. "Aren't you going to do something?"

Caleb smiled. "Yeah, I'm going to watch."

Josh dropped his hand from his face and fisted his hands at his sides. "Listen, I don't know what's going on. I don't know what you're talking about." A flicker of rage darkened his eyes. "But if you hit me again, I'm going to sue you and the whole town for abuse."

Benjamin jabbed him in the chin once again. "So, sue me."

"Turn around and put your hands behind your back," Caleb said. "Your partner in crime, Jeffrey Allen, is singing like a canary right now and you're under arrest for assault on Walt Tolliver and a bunch of other crimes that will be detailed later."

"Jeffrey Allen is a lying piece of crap," Josh exclaimed. "He's just trying to get away with everything he did."

"Turn around, Josh," Caleb repeated, his easygoing smile gone.

Josh looked at Benjamin, a small smile curving his lips. "Gee, hope you find what you're looking for." His gaze slid from Benjamin and to the cemetery in the distance.

It was a quick glance, almost imperceptible, but it shot a bolt of electricity through Benjamin, along with a horrifying sense of dread. "Get him downtown," Benjamin said just before he took off running.

"You're too late," Josh's voice rang out. "The bitch ruined everything. She's dead, Benjamin. You hear me? She's dead and buried."

Benjamin nearly stumbled as grief ripped through him. "No. No. No." The single word escaped him over and over again with each step he took.

Too late.

Too late.

The words thundered in his head and his grief was so intense he thought he might puke. The sun had sunk beneath the horizon and twilight had slammed in without warning.

The distance between him and the cemetery seemed agonizingly big. He ran so hard, so fast that a stitch in his side appeared.

Too late.

They'd all been too late for Brittany. They hadn't

known she was in trouble until she'd been gone for too long. They were probably too late for Jennifer Hightower and Suzy Bakersfield.

But this isn't the same case, he reminded himself. Edie wasn't one of the women who had disappeared without a trace. She'd been taken by Josh to punish her for destroying his dreams of wealth.

He released a sob as he flew through the cemetery entrance, his gaze seeking a fresh grave. It was not only grief that ripped through him but also a killing guilt.

They'd all told her it was over, that she was safe. They had taken Jeffrey's confession without asking the hard questions, without doubting the veracity. He'd put her in her car and sent her on her way. This was his fault.

He careened up and down the row of graves, seeking something that looked suspicious as darkness continued to fall. He'd always had a secret fear that he didn't have the capacity to feel deep emotion, to love with every fiber of his being. But as he hurried up and down the feet-worn paths between the graves, tears blurred his vision and he wished he couldn't feel.

He finally reached the end of the graves and didn't know whether to be relieved or disturbed that he'd found nothing. Where was she? Dear God, where could she be? He knew she was here somewhere, knew it with a sickening certainty.

Tom's patrol car pulled up, the lights of the vehicle cutting through the encroaching darkness. "Find her?" Tom asked as he hurried out of his car.

"No." The word worked around the lump in Benjamin's throat.

"Did you check the shed?"

Benjamin stared at him in confusion. "What shed?"

"Beyond that rise there's a little caretaker's shed." He pointed in the direction.

Benjamin took off running. He'd forgotten about the shed, which was tucked out of sight from the cemetery proper. He heard the sound of Tom's footsteps behind him and was grateful when his brother turned on a flashlight to light the way.

The old shed came into view and once again he felt like throwing up. *Please,* he begged. *Please let her be inside there. Please let her be okay.*

He tried not to think about all the places Josh could have buried her body. The cemetery was surrounded by land and he tried not to think about how long it might take before a burial site would be found.

Too late.

The words once again screamed in his head. *Please, please don't let me be too late.* He sent the prayer into the air and hoped that somebody was listening.

Darkness.

It surrounded her and invaded her soul. He'd said he'd come for her when it was dark, when nobody would see him bury her alive.

Her wrists were raw and bloody from working the ropes and the last piece of hope she'd entertained was gone. The darkness had arrived and the monster would arrive anytime.

Edie leaned her head back against the wall. Her head still hurt and she was more tired than she'd ever felt in her life. It seemed ridiculous that all this had happened because Poppy had thought he was seeing space aliens.

It also seemed ridiculous that she was going to be killed not because Josh wanted to protect himself, but because he was angry with her. Killing her was simply about revenge.

People were crazy, but she had been one of the craziest to walk away from Benjamin and love. "Love smart, Edie girl." Her grandmother's voice whispered through her head.

I did, Grandma. I loved smart when I fell in love with Benjamin and now it's too late for me, too late for us.

She stiffened and snapped her head upright as she heard the sound of running footsteps. He was coming. She closed her eyes and tried to become invisible in the darkness. A moan erupted from her as the door crashed open. She opened her eyes and saw only a dark shadow in the doorway.

Death. He had come for her.

"Edie."

She shivered at the voice that spoke her name, a cruel trick for he sounded like the man she loved.

Another body appeared in the doorway and a flashlight beam half blinded her. "Edie!" He rushed toward her and she realized it was Benjamin, not Josh.

She began to cry as he took the tape off her mouth. "It's okay, baby. It's all right. You're safe now. I promise you're safe." He pulled her forward into his arms as Tom got behind her and worked at the ropes that bound her.

"He said he was going to bury me alive," she cried as Benjamin held her tight. "He said I ruined his life so he was going to take mine."

When Tom freed her hands she wrapped her arms around Benjamin's neck, clinging to him as the fear slowly shuddered away.

Tom cut the rope that held her ankles and Benjamin scooped her up in his arms. "Let's get you out of here," he said as she buried her face into his broad chest.

The night was dark and cold, but she felt warm and safe in his arms as he carried her toward the house in the distance where the cars were parked.

"He drove up next to me," she said. "He motioned that something was wrong with my car. I was stupid to stop, but I thought it was safe." She clung tighter. "He told me my tire was going flat and when I bent over to look at it, he knocked me unconscious. I thought I was going to die."

When they reached the car, he placed her in the passenger seat and then hurried around to the driver's door. "Josh?" she asked as he slid in behind the steering wheel.

"Is in jail and I'm taking you to the hospital to get checked out."

She didn't argue with him. Her head pounded and her

wrists were encircled with dried blood from her attempts to get loose. "Why did Jeffrey confess to something he didn't do?"

"Josh threatened to kill Jeffrey's father if he talked," he said.

She leaned her head back against the seat and closed her eyes, trying to process everything that had happened, trying to forget how close she'd come to death. "How did you find me?" she asked, not opening her eyes.

"We leaned on Jeffrey and he came clean about Josh. Then I went to talk to Josh and leaned on him a bit."

She cracked an eye open and looked at him. "Leaned hard, I hope."

He smiled grimly. "I would have killed the bastard if Caleb hadn't been there."

She nodded and closed her eyes, satisfied with his reply. She was exhausted, her emotions a jumbled mess. The taste of horror still clung to the roof of her mouth and all she wanted to do was fall into a deep, dreamless sleep.

Two hours later her wrists had been treated and she'd been checked into a hospital room for a night of observation. "You and Walt are becoming familiar faces around here," Dr. Drake said when she was settled in a hospital bed. "You took quite a hit on the back of your head and I want to check those wrists again in the morning to make sure there's no infection setting in."

At that moment Benjamin appeared in the doorway. "I just brought Walt up to speed on everything. He said it's a good thing we arrested Josh, otherwise he would have had to release himself from here and kick his butt."

Edie gave him a weary smile. "That's my Poppy, ready to take on the bad guys and any space aliens that might invade his town."

"Get a good night's sleep, Edie," Dr. Drake said. "You've been through trauma and rest is the best medicine." He turned and gave Benjamin a stern look. "Don't you stress her with your questions. There's time enough to finish your investigation tomorrow."

"Don't worry, Doc. I'm just going to sit here for a little while until she falls asleep." As Dr. Drake left the room, Benjamin eased into a chair next to the hospital bed.

"You don't have to stay here," Edie protested as she fought to keep her eyes open.

"Yes, I do," he replied. "I need to sit here and watch you sleep. I need to assure myself that you're really okay. I just need to sit here and listen to you breathe." Emotion thickened his voice. "I've never been so afraid as when I saw your car parked on the side of the road. I don't ever want to be that afraid again."

She reached out a hand toward him and he grasped it in his. "I do love you, Benjamin," she said and then fell asleep.

She awakened to a sliver of early morning sun drifting through the window. Benjamin sat slumped in the chair, looking incredibly handsome and equally uncomfortable as he slept.

Her headache was gone and she felt ready to get out

of here, ready to face life with all its joy and with all its heartache.

As she looked at Benjamin her heart swelled as for the first time; she truly allowed herself to embrace all that was in her heart for him. Love. It fluttered through her with sweet warmth, filling up all the cold, empty places in her soul.

She gripped the charm around her neck and held tight. She would never forget the baby girl she'd lost, would always have an edge of grief where Mary was concerned. But she couldn't allow that tragedy to define who she was, to determine her future.

Benjamin's eyes fluttered open and for a moment she wanted to drown in the brown depths as he gazed at her. He straightened in the chair and quickly raked a hand through his tousled hair. "Good morning. How are you feeling?"

"Ready to get out of here and get on with my life," she replied.

"I had Tom take your car back to the ranch," he said as he stood. "I'll just get Dr. Drake in here and see if you're ready to be released."

Before she could stop him, he disappeared out the door. A niggle of doubt shot through her as she got up from the bed and headed for the bathroom.

Maybe he'd decided she was just too much trouble. He'd been emotional last night, but now he'd seemed a bit detached, as if he'd already moved on in his mind.

She changed into her clothes and checked her wrists, grateful that they looked less raw this morning. She finger-combed her hair and rinsed her mouth, then returned to the room to wait for Dr. Drake to come in and release her.

Benjamin came back through the door. "Looks like you're all ready to take off," he said as he leaned against the far wall.

"I told you, I'm ready for a fresh stab at life." She got up from the bed and took a step toward him.

He jammed his hands in his pockets, his expression unreadable. "You should be back on the road within an hour or so."

"Actually, I've been thinking about that. Being locked in that shed for hours, I did a lot of thinking." She took another step toward him, her heart suddenly beating almost painfully fast. "I thought about the fact that we've both suffered from loss, me with my daughter and you with your sister. I grieved for both of us and then realized how silly I'd been to try to protect myself from life…from love. I do love you, Benjamin, with all my heart."

His eyes lightened just a touch and he shoved himself off the wall. "Yeah, you told me that last night but I figured it was the result of whatever drug Dr. Drake might have given you."

She smiled. "He didn't give me any drugs. I meant what I said. I love you, and if it's not too late I want to be a part of your life. I didn't think I needed anyone, but I need you. I need my snuggle buddy."

He seemed to freeze in place. "Are you sure you don't

feel that way because I pulled you out of that shed? Because of some misplaced sense of gratitude?"

"Benjamin, I loved you when I got into my car to leave Black Rock. I loved you the night we made love. I feel like I was born loving you and that when I die, I'll feel the same way." She took another two steps forward, standing close enough to him that she could feel the heat radiating from him, smell the scent that made her think of warm male and home.

"I was afraid, that's why I was running away. I was afraid to believe that I deserved to be happy, but while I was sitting in that shed I knew I deserved happiness, that I deserve you."

He had her in his arms before her heart beat a second time. "I'll make you happy, Edie," he said and his eyes shone with a passion that nearly stole her breath away. "I love you, Edie, and I can't think of anyone I want more by my side for the rest of my life."

His lips descended on hers in a kiss that tasted of shared sunsets and fiery passion and love, sweet love. This was where she belonged, in Benjamin's life, in his strong arms.

When the kiss ended he reached out and touched the charm around her neck. "It's okay if you don't want to have children," he said. "I'll understand if that's what you choose."

He took her breath away. She knew that having a family was important to him and the fact that he was willing to make this sacrifice for her only spoke of the depth of his love.

She placed a hand on his cheek and smiled. "No way. We're going to fill that ranch house full of kids. Mary would have wanted lots of brothers and sisters."

He kissed her again and the kiss was interrupted by a deep clearing of a throat. They sprang apart to see Dr. Drake standing in the doorway. "Well, I guess I don't have to worry about her being in good hands," he said drily.

"Trust me, Doc, she's in the best of hands," Benjamin said as he pulled her against his side.

"Edie, you're good to go," Dr. Drake said.

"Great, then let's leave," she said to Benjamin. She was ready to start a new life with him.

They left the hospital and stepped out into the cool autumn morning sunshine. Once again Benjamin pulled her into his arms, his eyes filled with love and more than a touch of amusement. "I can't believe we owe all this to Walt and his space aliens."

"Maybe that means this was written in the stars," she said.

"So, you're willing to hitch your star to a full-time rancher?" he asked. "I'm not sure what I am without my badge."

She smiled up at him. "Oh, Benjamin, I'd hitch my star to you no matter what you did. I know what lies beneath your badge—a man with honor and compassion, the man I love with all my heart." She backed out of his arms. "Now, are you going to make me stand around in this hospital parking lot all day or are we going to the ranch and start practicing for those babies we're going to make?"

She laughed in delight as his eyes sparked with a fiery need and he tugged her toward his truck and into the future that she knew would be filled with laughter and passion and love.

Epilogue

"I still think we should have done corn bread stuffing," Poppy said as he and Margaret worked to stuff the giant Thanksgiving turkey.

"Sage dressing is traditional," Margaret said, her voice brooking no argument.

Edie smiled as she stood at the window and watched Benjamin as he approached the house from the pasture. It had been two months since the day she'd left the hospital, and in that two months much had occurred.

Benjamin had driven with her to Topeka to pack her belongings and bring them back to his place. Margaret had moved out of the cottage and into Poppy's house and the two seemed satisfied with their slightly contentious, but very caring companionship.

Benjamin still wore his badge, although he'd told his

brother that he was resigning in the spring. For Edie, the past two months had been magic. Her love for Benjamin had simply grown deeper, more profound, with each day that had passed.

All the facts of Josh's crimes had come to light. Jeffrey Allen was cooperating with authorities, hoping to get a lighter sentence when he came to trial.

Josh had provided the body parts for Jeffrey's experiments with the understanding that he would share in whatever proceeds Jeffrey eventually made. It had been Josh who had beaten Walt in the cemetery, an attempt to scare the old man into leaving things alone. It had also been Josh who had shot at them in the woods when he'd been burying the botched experiments.

Pure and simple it had been rage and greed that had driven Josh, and Edie was comforted by the fact that he would be in prison for a very long time to come.

Later this evening Tom and his fiancée, Peyton, were coming for dinner, as was Caleb and his fiancée, Portia. They had invited Jacob, but Benjamin had warned her that he probably wouldn't show up, that he'd prefer his isolation in the small cabin.

The front door opened and Benjamin came in, as always his face lighting up at the sight of her. He pulled her into his arms for a welcome kiss and then smiled as he heard Poppy and Margaret arguing about sweet potatoes. "I hear that our master chefs are at it again."

"At least we can be thankful to know that the dinner is probably going to be amazing," she replied.

"It will be nice to have everyone here," he said,

but his eyes darkened just a bit and she knew he was thinking about the two who would be missing—Jacob, who for some terrible reason that he refused to discuss had isolated himself from life, and of course, Brittany.

The darkness in his eyes lasted only a moment and then was gone, replaced by the light of love as he gazed at her. "I have a lot of things to be thankful for this year, and the main one is you."

As his lips met hers, her heart swelled with her own thanksgiving, happy that she'd been smart enough to open her heart to happiness, to love.

He was escalating his timeline.

When their captor brought in the fourth woman, Brittany realized the last two had been taken within a short span of time. She recognized the latest victim as Casey Teasdale, a young woman who worked as a receptionist in the dental office.

The masked man whistled as he carried the unconscious woman into the cell across from Brittany. Both Jennifer and Suzy went crazy at the sight of the new woman, one begging and the other cursing the man who held them.

Brittany sat silently, watching his every move, looking for something that might help her identify the man behind the mask. But as always, nothing he did led to an identification.

He locked the door of the cell where he'd placed Casey and then headed back toward the door of the barn where they were being kept. He stopped in front of Brittany's enclosure and she felt his sick energy, his excitement as he looked at her.

"Almost time," he said. "I only need to add one more to my collection and then the games will begin." He began to whistle again as he left the building.

Brittany stared after him, knowing that time was running out for her, that time was running out for them all.

* * * * *

COMING NEXT MONTH

Available January 25, 2011

SRSCNM0111

REQUEST YOUR FREE BOOKS!

2 FREE NOVELS PLUS 2 FREE GIFTS!

ROMANTIC SUSPENSE

Sparked by Danger, Fueled by Passion.

YES! Please send me 2 FREE Silhouette® Romantic Suspense novels and my 2 FREE gifts (gifts are worth about $10). After receiving them, if I don't wish to receive any more books, I can return the shipping statement marked "cancel." If I don't cancel, I will receive 4 brand-new novels every month and be billed just $4.24 per book in the U.S. or $4.99 per book in Canada. That's a saving of 15% off the cover price! It's quite a bargain! Shipping and handling is just 50¢ per book.* I understand that accepting the 2 free books and gifts places me under no obligation to buy anything. I can always return a shipment and cancel at any time. Even if I never buy another book from Silhouette, the two free books and gifts are mine to keep forever.

240/340 SDN E5Q4

Name	(PLEASE PRINT)
Address	Apt. #
City	State/Prov.	Zip/Postal Code

Signature (if under 18, a parent or guardian must sign)

Mail to the **Silhouette Reader Service:**
IN U.S.A.: P.O. Box 1867, Buffalo, NY 14240-1867
IN CANADA: P.O. Box 609, Fort Erie, Ontario L2A 5X3

Not valid for current subscribers to Silhouette Romantic Suspense books.

Want to try two free books from another line?
Call 1-800-873-8635 or visit www.morefreebooks.com.

* Terms and prices subject to change without notice. Prices do not include applicable taxes. N.Y. residents add applicable sales tax. Canadian residents will be charged applicable provincial taxes and GST. Offer not valid in Quebec. This offer is limited to one order per household. All orders subject to approval. Credit or debit balances in a customer's account(s) may be offset by any other outstanding balance owed by or to the customer. Please allow 4 to 6 weeks for delivery. Offer available while quantities last.

Your Privacy: Silhouette is committed to protecting your privacy. Our Privacy Policy is available online at www.eHarlequin.com or upon request from the Reader Service. From time to time we make our lists of customers available to reputable third parties who may have a product or service of interest to you. If you would prefer we not share your name and address, please check here. ☐

Help us get it right—We strive for accurate, respectful and relevant communications. To clarify or modify your communication preferences, visit us at www.ReaderService.com/consumerschoice.

*Harlequin Romance author Donna Alward is loved
for her gorgeous rancher heroes.*

*Meet Wyatt as he's confronted by both a precious
little pink bundle left on his doorstep and his neighbor Elli
who's going to show him the ropes....*

Introducing
PROUD RANCHER, PRECIOUS BUNDLE

THE SQUAWKING QUIETED as Elli picked the baby up, and
Wyatt turned around, trying hard to ignore the feelings of
inadequacy as Darcy immediately stopped fussing.

"Maybe she's uncomfortable. What do you think, sweet-
heart?" Elli turned her conversation to the baby.

"What do you think is wrong?" Wyatt asked, putting the
coffee pot back on the burner.

A strange look passed over Elli's face, one that looked
like guilt and panic. But it was gone quickly. "I couldn't
say," she replied.

"But you were so good with her this afternoon." Wyatt
put his hands on his hips.

"Lucky, that's all. I just…remembered a few things."
The same strange look flitted over her features once more.

Wyatt took the coffee to the table. "You fooled me. You
looked like you knew exactly what you were doing." So
much so that Wyatt had felt completely inept. A feeling he
despised. He was used to being the one in control.

Elli and Darcy walked the length of the kitchen and
back. After a few moments, she admitted, "I haven't really
cared for a baby before. The things I thought of were simply
things I'd heard about. Not from experience, Mr. Black."

Her chin jutted up, closing the subject but making him

want to ask the questions now pulsing through his mind. But then he remembered the old saying—*Don't look a gift horse in the mouth.* He'd benefit from whatever insight she had and be glad of it.

"I don't really know what babies need," he said. "I fed her, patted her back like you did, walked her to sleep, but every time I put her down…"

Wyatt almost groaned. Of course. He'd forgotten one important thing. He'd been so focused on getting the formula the right temperature that he'd forgotten to check her diaper. Not that he had any clue what to do there either.

Pulling calves and shoveling out stalls was far less intimidating than one tiny newborn.

"She's probably due for a diaper change, isn't she." He tried to sound nonchalant. This was a perfect opportunity. Elli must know how to change a diaper. He could simply watch her so he'd know better for the next time.

Instead, Elli came around the corner of the counter and placed Darcy back in his arms. "Here you go, Uncle Wyatt," she said lightly. "You get diaper duty. I'll fix the coffee. Cream and sugar?"

Oh boy, Wyatt thought, looking down into Darcy's pursed face, his smug plan blown to smithereens. He was in for it now.

Will sparks fly between Elli and Wyatt?

Find out in
PROUD RANCHER, PRECIOUS BUNDLE
Available February 2011 from Harlequin Romance

Try these Healthy and Delicious Spring Rolls!

INGREDIENTS

2 packages rice-paper
spring roll wrappers
(20 wrappers)

1 cup grated carrot

¼ cup bean sprouts

1 cucumber, julienned

1 red bell pepper, without
stem and seeds, julienned

4 green onions
finely chopped—
use only the green part

DIRECTIONS

1. Soak one rice-paper wrapper
   in a large bowl of hot water
   until softened.

2. Place a pinch each of carrots,
   sprouts, cucumber, bell
   pepper and green onion on the
   wrapper toward the bottom
   third of the rice paper.

3. Fold ends in and roll tightly
   to enclose filling.

4. Repeat with remaining
   wrappers. Chill before
   serving.

Find this and many more delectable recipes
including the perfect dipping sauce in

HARLEQUIN *Presents*

USA TODAY bestselling author

Sharon Kendrick

introduces

HIS MAJESTY'S CHILD

The king's baby of shame!

King Casimiro harbors a secret—no one in the kingdom
of Zaffirinthos knows that a devastating accident has left
his memory clouded in darkness. And Casimiro himself
cannot answer why Melissa Maguire, an enigmatic English
rose, stirs such feelings in him…. Questioning his ability
to rule, Casimiro decides he will renounce the throne.
But Melissa has news she knows will rock the palace
to its core—*Casimiro has an heir!*

Law dictates Casimiro cannot abdicate, so he must find a
way to reacquaint himself with Melissa—his new queen!

Available from Harlequin Presents
February 2011

Silhouette **Desire**

USA TODAY bestselling author

ELIZABETH BEVARLY

**is back with a steamy
and powerful story.**

Gavin Mason is furious and vows revenge on
high-price, high-society girl Violet Tandy.
Her novel is said to be fiction, but everyone
knows she's referring to Gavin as a client in
her memoir. The tension builds when they
learn not to judge a book by its cover.

THE BILLIONAIRE GETS HIS WAY

*Available February
wherever books are sold.*

Always Powerful, Passionate and Provocative.

Visit Silhouette Books at www.eHarlequin.com

SD73078

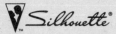

Sparked by Danger, Fueled by Passion.

NEW YORK TIMES BESTSELLING AUTHOR

RACHEL LEE

No Ordinary Hero

Strange noises...a woman's mysterious disappearance
and a killer on the loose who's too close for comfort.

With no where else to turn, Delia Carmody looks
to her aloof neighbour to help, only to discover
that Mike Windwalker is no ordinary hero.

Available in February.
Wherever books are sold.